Nedrick Quittor answers the phone expecting to hear that his buddy, Rierdon, is running late because he always seems to run late. That's true today, too, as Rierdon's truck broke down, and he's stranded.

Ready to laugh and tell his friend I told you so because Nedrick had warned Rierdon to fix the problem over a week ago, he heads to the campground where his friend is waiting. After confirming the truck needs a tow, he's approached by the sweetest-smelling human he's ever encountered — Brett. Nedrick is momentarily shocked to discover that his mate, the other half of his soul, just walked up to him.

In the course of helping him, Nedrick learns that Brett's there camping with friends . . . and one of them, Karissa, is dating him and already has designs on his mate. On the plus side, he discovers that Brett's already friends with a few of his pack-members. The human just doesn't know it.

With a little help from his friends, can Nedrick steal his human without revealing the existence of shifters to those who'd use that knowledge against them?

Stealing his Human
Copyright © 2024 Charlie Richards
ISBN: 978-1-4874-3510-3
Cover art by Martine Jardin

Published by eXtasy Books Inc

Look for us online at:
www.eXtasybooks.com

STEALING HIS HUMAN
WOLVES OF STONE RIDGE: BOOK SIXTY-THREE

BY

CHARLIE RICHARDS

DEDICATION

To my amazing editor, Officer Laura, for everything this fantastic lady does for me!

CHAPTER ONE

"Hey, Rierdon." Nedrick Quittor smirked as he answered his phone, greeting his friend. "Running late again?"

His fellow wolf shifter and friend of nearly eighty years always seemed to be running late. It was a good thing the man didn't have the standard nine-to-five job. He would've never been able to hold it down.

Instead, Rierdon was a sculptor, working with metal to turn what Nedrick saw as random pieces of scrap into works of art. Nedrick had no idea how Rierdon did it, but he had to admit, his buddy had a gift. His pieces sold online for hundreds and thousands of dollars, depending on the size and scope of the piece.

Perhaps that's why he's always late. His mind's busy working on his next piece of art.

Being somewhere on time just wasn't important enough to stick in his brain.

Considering nearly everyone in their wolf shifter pack knew of Rierdon's inability to be punctual, no one ended up upset about it. Even their alpha, Declan McIntire, would smile indulgently when Rierdon showed up thirty minutes late for a pack barbeque. His friend would grin sheepishly, duck his head, and blush. Then he would rush to the food because, of course, he would be starving.

Guess forgetting to eat landed right in there with being punctual.

"Uh, well, yeah," Rierdon replied. His voice sounded more stressed than usual, putting Nedrick on alert. "Well, ya see—"

1

"Hey, don't sweat it, Rierdon," Nedrick rumbled, doing his best to soothe his friend. Having been relaxing on his front porch swing with a sweating glass of iced tea while waiting for his friend, he lifted a bare foot to the railing in front of him and began a slow swinging. "There's no rush, man. Ya get here when ya get here."

Being a lazy Saturday afternoon, Nedrick had the entire day off. He worked as a mechanic at Kade McGraw's shop. When the fellow wolf shifter had earned an enforcer position with the pack nearly a decade before, he'd hired a few more people. His duties for the pack often took him away from his work, and with the town growing, Kade had been smart to expand his workforce. His boss's shop had a fantastic reputation, and people from other nearby towns would come to him, too.

"It's not that I'm just late," Rierdon stated with a sigh. "I'm, uh . . . my truck broke down."

"Your truck broke down?" Nedrick moved his foot back to the porch planking and straightened. "What happened? Are you okay?"

Rierdon sounded so dejected when he replied, "Yeah, I'm okay. Just . . . embarrassed." He groaned out his next words. "You warned me."

"The tie-rod ends?" Nedrick guessed, doing his best to hide his laughter. He had indeed warned his friend. Nedrick had borrowed Rierdon's truck to move a sofa just the prior week and had heard the telltale thuds when going over a few potholes in his driveway.

I need to fix those, too, come to think of it.

"Yeah." Rierdon heaved a put-upon sigh. "At least, I made it into the campground."

"Which campground?" Nedrick rose to his feet and headed into his cabin. "Maybe I can cobble something together to get you to town and the shop."

"I really appreciate it, Ned," Rierdon stated, then told him he was at Tall Timbers Campground. "I know this isn't how you wanted to spend your Saturday."

Nedrick grabbed a pair of jeans from his dresser drawer and tossed them on the bed. "No worries, Rier. Life happens, and that's what friends are for," he countered. Pulling out socks next, he admitted, "I'll need a few to get dressed. Then I'll hit the road. I should be there in twenty."

"Thanks, Ned." Rierdon sounded so relieved. "I appreciate it."

"You're welcome. See you soon."

Nedrick closed the call and tossed his phone on the bed beside his clothes. After shucking his jogging shorts, the only thing he'd had on, he quickly began to dress. Nedrick had been waiting for Rierdon to arrive so they could shift into their wolves and go running through the trees together.

Sensing his wolf's disappointment, Nedrick soothed his inner animal by promising him a moonlit run instead. Mollified, his beast accepted the change of plans and relaxed within him.

While Nedrick — and most shifters in general — considered them and their animals to be one and the same, they each had slightly different instincts. Keeping both sides of their nature in harmony was a balancing act. Nedrick had watched his mother try to deny her wolf, and she'd almost ended up losing herself to her animal side.

That was when Nedrick had been young, and for a long while, he'd feared his nature. His alpha had uncovered what was going on and helped his mother recover. Declan had also explained to Nedrick what had happened, and he'd taught him their true nature and how to balance both sides of himself.

Nedrick would forever be grateful to Alpha Declan, and he couldn't imagine living under any other alpha's leadership.

After grabbing his keys, Nedrick strode out the door, ready

to help his friend . . . and maybe tell him *I told you so.*

Arriving at Tall Timbers Campground, Nedrick turned into the lane. He spotted the small guard shack ahead, but he didn't see the ranger who was supposed to be manning it. Rolling by slowly, Nedrick searched the area ahead of him.

The road split into three directions. The one to the right had an arrow indicating you could drive in that direction, as did the one straight ahead. The road to the left had an arrow pointing toward him, as well as a no-entrance sign.

Knowing the campgrounds were set up with one-way loops—and surely Rierdon couldn't have gotten too far—Nedrick veered to the right. He immediately spotted his friend's truck parked in a camp spot amidst the trees. Not only was Rierdon standing near the back bumper, but so was Wraith Urdman. The man was a fellow wolf shifter and in uniform, which told Nedrick that he was the one on duty.

Wraith had probably helped Rierdon park his truck, too. Even though Rierdon was a wolf shifter, he was on the smaller side, standing five-foot-ten with a lithe build. His black wolf was sleek and swift, but not very large.

On the other hand, the ranger had the more common buff-like build and stood at six-foot-two.

Nedrick knew that he was somewhere in the middle. While he topped six feet, standing six-foot-one, his build was leaner than the large forest ranger. He didn't mind, though. With his muscular frame, Nedrick had never had any trouble finding companionship for the night on the rare occasion that he went looking.

Parking his *Jeep* off to the side behind Rierdon's truck so he didn't block the flow of traffic, Nedrick greeted the other wolf shifters. "Hey, Rier, Wraith." He eyed the way the left front tire of the truck veered toward the left. Shaking his head, he recalled how the truck's other front tire had been positioned straight ahead. "That had to be a beast to park."

Wraith chuckled, his smile rueful, while Nedrick ducked his head and blushed. "We made do," Wraith told him, watching Nedrick as he jumped from his vehicle. "He said he called you for a lift or tow." Eyeing Nedrick's vehicle speculatively, he told him, "Not sure that's going to do the job, though."

"Gonna see if I can jury rig it first," Nedrick explained as he pulled a jack from the back of his *Jeep*. As he crossed to the truck, he admitted, "Although, from seeing it now, I doubt I'll be able to." Nedrick lowered to his knees. "I'll probably have to zip over to Kade's garage and hook up the dolly."

Wraith nodded, his attention straying to a vehicle that was turning into the entrance. "Good luck, Ned." He patted him on the shoulder before striding swiftly back to the park's small office. As Wraith hurried away, the black-haired shifter mumbled, "You're gonna need it."

"Thanks," Nedrick quipped back with a chuckle.

"Thanks again, Ned," Rierdon murmured, standing at his shoulder with his arms wrapped around his torso. He nibbled his bottom lip and stared at his cock-eyed wheel with an expression of impending doom. "I appreciate you comin'."

Hating to see his normally happy-go-lucky buddy so down in the dumps, Nedrick patted him on the shin. "Like I said, Rierdon." He grinned up at the smaller shifter. "That's what friends are for." After carefully peering around the tire, Nedrick confirmed his fear. "Yep. This ain't goin' nowhere without a tow." Nedrick lowered the truck tire back to the ground and stood, giving Rierdon a warm smile. "Looks like we're gonna have to make a trip to Kade's garage."

Rierdon sighed heavily. "Sorry for ruining your day."

"You haven't ruined my day," Nedrick countered, resting his hand on the back of Rierdon's neck and squeezing lightly in reassurance. "This is just a speedbump. We'll—"

"Hey, guys," a deep voice called, drawing Nedrick's attention to the approaching man. "I hate to ask, but could I borrow your jack?" The stranger pointed at the jack Nedrick had left on the ground. The handsome guy appeared rueful as he continued toward them, rubbing the back of his neck in obvious discomfort. "My car's got a flat, and damned if none of us have a jack on us."

"Yeah, sure," Nedrick replied, not minding lending a quick hand. "Where are you" — the man was finally close enough for the guy's scent to reach him, and Nedrick drew in a sharp gasp as the human's intoxicating aroma teased his senses, before he softly finished — "parked."

The stranger's masculine goodness filled Nedrick's nostrils, making his mouth water. The hairs on his arms stood on end, and his belly suddenly felt as if it was filled with butterflies. His heart began racing in his chest as the human stopped before him.

Holy shit! My mate is standing in front of me. Holy shit, holy shit, holy shit!

Sweeping his gaze over the human, Nedrick admired his thick, slightly curly auburn hair. It had been cut in waves, giving him a boyish, windswept look that made Nedrick want to run his fingers through it. The human stood the same height as Nedrick, six-foot-one, and had wider shoulders that would be fantastic for holding onto while he ravished his mouth.

When Rierdon nudged him discreetly, Nedrick blinked, realizing that he'd been staring and hadn't heard a thing his mate had been saying.

Great first impression, Ned.

Mentally chastising himself, Nedrick cleared his throat and smiled. "Uh, sorry." He gave his mate another quick once-over, wishing he had time to really check out the man who was the other half of his soul, but the guy was already looking at him as if he were nuts. Nedrick didn't want to make an even worse first impression. "Did you want to hop in my *Jeep*?

I can drive us to your campsite?"

Nedrick assumed the guy was there camping, since he was pretty darn certain the human wasn't from the area.

"Oh, uh, sure," the man replied, sounding a little uncertain. He seemed to rally quickly, a small smile curving his thin lips. "Sounds good."

Grabbing his jack, Nedrick opened the back of his *Jeep* and placed it inside. He couldn't help continuing to discreetly glance at the human every few seconds — *my mate*. After shutting the door, Nedrick indicated his vehicle. "Hop in."

As Nedrick's mate grabbed a roll bar and athletically hopped into the back, Rierdon grabbed Nedrick's wrist, stopping him from climbing behind the wheel. "You all right?" he whispered, his brows furrowed in concern.

"I'm *great*," Nedrick murmured back, grinning broadly at his friend. "Best damn day of my life." Upon seeing the way Rierdon's brows shot up and scenting his surprise, Nedrick jerked his chin in the human's direction. "He's my mate."

Rierdon gaped for a few seconds before snapping his mouth shut again and hissing, "Brett's your mate?"

"Brett?" Nedrick repeated softly, his gut warming at the knowledge. "His name is Brett? You know him?"

Rolling his eyes, Rierdon shook his head as he released him. "No, I don't know him," he mumbled as he took a step away from Nedrick. "He introduced himself as Brett Robinson." As Rierdon moved farther away, rounding the hood of the *Jeep*, only Nedrick's shifter hearing allowed him to hear his friend's mumbled, "Damn, you were really zoned out there."

Nedrick couldn't argue with that. Hopping behind the wheel, he brought his vehicle to life. "Okay, Brett." He smiled, enjoying the strong short name as it rolled off his tongue. With a glance over his shoulder, Nedrick put his vehicle into gear. "Let me know where to stop."

Seeing Brett nod, Nedrick eased off the brake and started them along the one-way loop.

Reaching the end of that one, Brett pointed straight ahead. "We're on that loop, near the back."

Nedrick nodded and headed that way. "Out of curiosity," he began, just because he wanted to hear Brett's rich tenor once more. "If you're back here, how'd you see me and my jack?"

Brett shrugged. "I was walking to the guard shack to see if the ranger had a jack in his truck. Spotted you with him." He pointed again. "That's us."

Looking where Brett pointed, Nedrick immediately saw the older *GMC Envoy* with the rear flat tire. The hatch door was raised, and it was obvious that Brett had been searching the interior. Nedrick barely resisted smirking because, really, why wouldn't his mate have the jack with him? Especially since he was going into the mountains camping?

I'll just thank Fate for that little oversight.

As they approached and slowed, Nedrick noticed three other people approaching from around a hatchback *Ford Focus*—two women and a man. A short-haired brunette had an arm wrapped proprietarily around the blond man's waist, and he reciprocated with his arm around her shoulders. The second woman, a redhead with her hair piled on the top of her head in an artfully messy bun, looked over the occupants of his *Jeep* and immediately smiled welcomingly . . . at Brett.

The woman skip-bounced a couple of steps forward, then slowed as some random thought crossed her pretty features—as if catching herself. "Hey, Brett," she greeted him, completely ignoring Nedrick and Rierdon as he parked his *Jeep*. *Huh.* Her smile could only be called flirty as she continued, "Any luck?"

Oh, hell, no.

Nedrick realized this woman was anything but subtle. If she wasn't already dating Brett, she was angling to be.

Not going to happen.

Feeling his wolf growl in his mind, Nedrick completely agreed with his beast.

Or if they are dating, I'll be putting a stop to it quick, fast, and in a hurry. Brett is mine.

"Hey, Karissa," Brett greeted with a small smile of his own. As Nedrick shut off his *Jeep*, he couldn't help but notice the way his mate scented a bit of appreciation as he eyed her — Karissa — while saying, "This is Ned and his friend, Rierdon. Ned has a jack I can borrow."

"Awesome." Karissa beamed a smile at Brett as if he were the second coming of Christ. "I knew you'd figure it out," she gushed. Finally, Karissa turned her attention to Nedrick and Rierdon, her expression immediately changing almost to disinterest. "Thanks, guys. We sure appreciate it." When Karissa turned her attention back to Brett, she grinned again. "Now we can go on that hike we talked about."

"Yeah." Brett rose from his seat and hopped over the side of the *Jeep*. "That's the plan."

Nedrick followed in time to see Karissa latch both hands onto one of Brett's arms and press her breasts to his chest. "It'll be so much fun," she gushed, peering up at him through her lashes. "I hear there's a great scenic spot for a picnic." Her voice lowered seductively. "And it's secluded."

Brett cleared his throat as he glanced around, looking decidedly uncomfortable.

Good.

"Well, uh." Brett had to practically peel Karissa's hands from his arm as he stated, "I better get my tire changed, then."

Nedrick took that as his cue to head to the back of his *Jeep*. As he moved, he did his best to keep a muscle from ticking in his jaw.

"Keep your cool, man," Rierdon urged, gripping his upper arm to get his attention. "We'll help fix this, but you can't go off half-cocked on this one."

Knowing Rierdon was right, Nedrick jerked a nod. "Thanks, man."

With that thought in mind and knowing his pack would help him, Nedrick began plotting on how to steal his human mate.

CHAPTER TWO

After peeling Karissa's hands from his upper arm, Brett Robinson barely fought back the urge to massage his bicep. The woman had been clutching way too tightly. Brett had never seen her act so overtly possessive.

We're not even really a couple, yet. Geez. And why? I brought back a couple of guys.

Brett had taken Karissa out on two dates, each of the last two Friday evenings. According to Tyler—the buddy Brett was there camping with—Tyler's girlfriend, Tabatha, had known Karissa for a couple of years. Evidently, Karissa had seen Brett's picture on Tabatha's phone and had wanted to meet him.

Brett had found it flattering. Plus, after seeing Karissa's picture, he'd thought she was pretty. While he'd been a little worried about her living up to her red hair's stigma, until right then, Brett hadn't noticed any overly fiery personality.

Maybe it's because I turned down her offer to share a tent last night.

While Brett knew Tyler expected him to bed Karissa on their camping trip, he hadn't decided if he wanted to take that step with her. He wasn't ruled by his dick, after all. Considering Karissa had been friends with Tabatha for a couple of years, if Brett slept with her and it didn't work out, it could not only mess up the girls' friendship, but Brett's own friendship with Tyler.

As often as Brett had heard the adage *bros before hoes*, he didn't think that would fly in this case. Tyler loved Tabatha dearly. In fact, Brett knew his buddy had bought a ring and was planning to pop the question at some point this trip.

Maybe I shouldn't have agreed to invite Karissa camping. She's gonna get ideas that I'm so not ready for.

Settling down and getting married wasn't even a blip on Brett's radar right then. He had one more year of college, and focusing on his studies took plenty of his time. Brett realized he probably shouldn't have even agreed to that first date with Karissa.

Hindsight sucks.

Following Nedrick to his GMC's rear wheel, Brett watched the wiry Good Samaritan slide the jack under his vehicle's frame. Then he fitted one of the sockets of the four-way tire iron onto a lug nut. With a wrench that made it look easy, Nedrick loosened the nut.

"Hey, when I asked to borrow your jack," Brett began, touching the man's shoulder to get his attention. When the man's intense brown-eyed gaze lifted and pinned on him, Brett felt his mouth go dry. Not understanding the odd reaction, he quickly swallowed before finishing, "I didn't mean for you to change it for me."

Nedrick grinned widely, his eyes appearing to twinkle. "Happy to help, mate," he responded and even winked. "I'm a mechanic. I'll have this off swift, fast, and in a hurry for ya." Then Nedrick gripped Brett's calf and squeezed gently. "Why don't ya pull out your spare?"

Brett jerked a nod, surprised to find the hairs on his shorts-clad leg lifting from the feel of Nedrick's palm on him. Even the skin on his leg began to goose bump. "Uh, o-okay." Confused by his body's reaction, Brett pulled away to do just that.

As Brett reached into the rear cargo area of his vehicle, he tried to figure out what the hell was going on with him. He'd never had a reaction like that from a smile and touch from a guy. It was . . . odd.

More than a little, actually.

Deciding to dismiss it, since Brett didn't understand it, he slid a cooler over to the right. He focused on easing the tire out of the well under the cargo area. Brett flexed his arms and grunted, dragging it forward.

"Can I help?"

Karissa's perky voice came from Brett's left, startling him. He felt the tire slip from the fingers of his left hand. The tire rotated, pulling from his right hand's grip. The heavy object banged back into the well, pinning his fingers between it and the well's metal side.

"Shit," Brett hissed, yanking his hand free. Pain radiated through his pointer and index fingers. He gripped his right wrist with his left hand and peered at it. Seeing blood oozing from a gash in the tip of his index finger, Brett grimaced, closed his eyes, and blew out a breath. "Damn it," he muttered, trying to ease his racing pulse.

Brett had never been good with the sight of blood, much to Tyler's amusement. His buddy had teased him aplenty about it.

Good thing I don't plan to go into the medical field.

"Oh, no!" Karissa whined, grabbing his left forearm. "I'm so sorry. I didn't mean to startle you."

"Hey, you okay?"

Brett heard Nedrick's question, but he was too busy focusing on his breathing — and controlling the pulsing pain in his hand — to respond.

"Damn," Nedrick murmured, gripping his wrist lightly. "Let me take a look."

Feeling Nedrick's strong fingers lift his arm, Brett released his own hold and just went with it. He felt his pulse slowing as the pain began to ease. Brett knew he would need to suck it up and clean the wound, but he needed another few seconds.

When Brett felt warm lips wrap around his bleeding digit, he snapped his eyes open. Shock rushed through him at the sight before him. Nedrick had stuck Brett's finger into his mouth, and he stared at him with calm reassurance in his brown eyes.

The heat of Nedrick's mouth, coupled with the feel of the guy's soft tongue gently lapping at his fingertip, shot a strange bolt of warmth straight to his gut. He felt his stomach clench, and he sucked in a sharp gasp.

Brett stared at Nedrick for a heartbeat, two, before gathering his scattered wits about him. "What the —" he began, tugging lightly, but Nedrick didn't release him.

Instead, Nedrick winked and smiled around Brett's finger while sliding his tongue over the tip of his digit again. The move caused the fluttering in his belly to morph into something hotter, which traveled south. To Brett's surprise, he felt his prick begin to chub up.

Karissa whining, "Ewww, that's disgusting," yanked Brett out of his shocked stupor.

Brett jerked his hand away from Nedrick with more force, and the other man released him with a grin and a shrug. The man cut his attention to Karissa and claimed, "When I get a cut, and my finger's hurting, the first thing I do is stick it in my mouth. Don't you?"

"W-Well —" Karissa blustered, her cheeks darkening a bit.

Nedrick continued, obviously not interested in her answer, turning his attention back to Brett. "And with how pale you suddenly got and started some deep breathing exercises, along with the way you gripped your wrist . . ." His lips curved into a smile that appeared understanding. "I figured you weren't going to do it yourself, so I decided to help you out." Reaching out, Nedrick rested his hand on Brett's shoulder and squeezed lightly. "Not so good with blood, mate?"

Clearing his throat, Brett shook his head. "Not so much." He took a chance and peered at his hand since the throbbing had ebbed drastically. "Huh." To his surprise, the gash didn't look nearly as bad as he'd originally thought, and the bleeding had already stopped. "Well, that's —"

Before Brett could finish with *strange*, Nedrick squeezed his shoulder once more and asked, "Feeling better now?"

"Yeah, actually, I —"

"Well, *I* still think it's disgusting," Karissa cut in, reasserting herself into the conversation. She gave his forearm a little squeeze, reminding Brett that she continued to clutch him. "Are you going to be okay to hike?"

"Yeah, of course," Brett replied, frowning when he watched Nedrick turn and grab the tire. "My hand'll be just fine."

"Oh, good." Karissa beamed at him as if he'd just given her the best news ever. Peering at him from beneath her lashes, she whispered in a sultry tone, "Because I can't wait to enjoy some nature with you."

The loud sound of the tire slamming on asphalt drew both their attention. Out of the corner of his eye, Brett noticed Karissa's narrowed eyes and annoyed expression. He began to think she saw Nedrick as competition, but he couldn't understand why that would be.

Brett watched as Nedrick flashed a smile his way before wheeling the tire around the side of his *Envoy*. "Where are you planning to hike?" he asked, glancing back at him. "I've been all over these mountains. Is there some sight you'd like to see?" Lifting the tire into place — the flat one was already off to the side — Nedrick made it look easy, and he kept talking. "Waterfalls? Meadows? Wildlife? Expansive views? We got 'em all here."

Realizing he was letting Nedrick change his tire and he wasn't even helping, Brett pulled from Karissa's clingy grip. "Uh, well, we'll be here through all next week, so we're hoping to enjoy all that," he admitted. Grabbing a lug nut from the ground, he offered it to Nedrick when he began looking.

"So, yeah. Any advice on trails would be great."

Nedrick took the nut slowly, sliding his thumb over Brett's in the process in a move that felt surprisingly like a caress. "I'll do you one better, mate," Nedrick told him with a warm smile. "I'll show you all that and more."

Did that sound suggestive?

Naw, that can't be right.

"We have a map of the trails," Karissa claimed, teasing her fingers through Brett's hair. Her touch caused a shiver to work down his back, and the hairs on his neck stood on end, and not in a pleasant way. "So I think we can find our own way, thanks."

Nedrick flicked his gaze up to where Karissa threaded her fingers through Brett's hair before refocusing on Brett's face. His eyes appeared to twitch for just an instant. Then he shrugged, took another lug nut from Brett, and focused on fitting it to the tire.

"Well, the offer stands," Nedrick stated.

"Ned, what are you doing here?"

Brett turned and stood, spotting Preall McCollins approaching. The large, blond-haired man held the hand of his fiancée—Trina Truollo. He'd met Trina his freshman year in college when they'd shared a couple of classes, and she'd introduced them. Brett had been surprised at the apparent age gap between her and her *boyfriend*—who looked to be in his thirties while Trina was only eighteen at the time—but it hadn't taken him long to realize they were a solid couple. Trina was also the reason they'd chosen to camp in the mountains near Stone Ridge. She'd raved about the area, which was where she'd met Preall and had been encouraging them for the last couple of years to come check it out.

"Hey, Preall," Nedrick greeted with a grin, rising to his feet. He reached over and clasped Preall's hand, and they shared a quick, one-armed bro-hug. Stepping back and releasing him, Nedrick indicated Brett. "Just changin' the tire of my new mate, Brett, here."

While Preall nodded slowly, the corners of his lips quirking just a smidge, Brett noticed that Trina's eyes widened quite a bit. She even looked up at Preall, who met her gaze with a smile. Then the big man lifted their twined hands and pecked a kiss to the back of hers before returning his attention to Nedrick.

"Well, that's awful nice of you, Ned," Preall stated, glancing at the tire. "You'll have to join us hiking while our friends are up here."

"I'd enjoy that," Nedrick replied with a grin. "You know I always enjoy hiking." Then he glanced toward his buddy, Rierdon, and added, "And I was actually here to check out Rierdon's truck. It broke down."

Preall smiled at Rierdon. "Hey, man." After offering Rierdon the same greeting as Nedrick, he grimaced and said, "Sorry to hear about your truck."

Rierdon's smile appeared wry. "It's fixable."

With a nod, Preall returned his attention to Nedrick, who'd returned to changing out the tire. He'd lowered the jack and picked up the four-way wrench once more. After giving each lug a couple more twists, Nedrick picked up his jack and straightened.

Nedrick tucked the jack under his left arm, holding the iron in that same hand. "I'll see you again before too long, Brett," he claimed, holding out his hand to him.

Not wanting to appear rude and wondering about the undercurrents that were passing between these guys, Brett took Nedrick's hand. "Sure." He felt the other man squeeze lightly while rubbing his thumb over the back of his hand twice before releasing him.

Then Nedrick nodded at Karissa and the others, saying, "Nice to meet y'all," before patting Rierdon on the shoulder. "Come on, Rier," he urged, heading toward his *Jeep*. "Let's go get that dolly and get your truck to the shop."

Rierdon opened his mouth before snapping it shut just as quickly and following Nedrick to his vehicle. After the guy had put away his tools, he climbed behind the wheel, and Rierdon joined him in the passenger seat. He fired up the engine.

"I'll keep you posted on where we'll be," Preall told him with a wave. "Trina and I'll set up camp, then decide." He pointed at the campsite right next to where Brett and the others were.

"Thanks, Pre," Nedrick called before heading away.

Brett watched Nedrick drive away and found he actually looked forward to seeing him again. For some reason, he enjoyed the friendly mechanic's presence. The guy could make a great friend.

His attention was quickly averted by Karissa once more as she demanded scathingly, "Why are you going to invite him, Preall?" She scowled at him while resting her hands on her hips. "It's so damn obvious that he's after Brett. He's trying to poach my guy."

"Wait, what?" Brett looked from Karissa to Preall, sure that his friend would deny that. "He was just being nice."

Preall scoffed as he released Trina's hand in order to wrap his arm around her waist. "Well, I can tell you that Ned would have changed your tire without being interested in you. That's just the kind of stand-up guy he is." Then he smirked at Brett as he indicated Karissa. "But Karissa's right. He *is* interested in you." With a laugh, Preall winked. "How could you not notice his flirting?"

"Yeah?" Karissa snapped, turning to frown at Brett. "How come you didn't notice and set him straight?" She stepped close and pressed her breasts to his side as she gripped his arm again. "You're with me, and you're not interested."

Confusion flooded him even as he fought his desire to extricate himself from Karissa's clinginess.

Before Brett had a chance to dig up a response, Tyler barked a laugh. "Hell, Brett wouldn't notice a guy bein' interested if he walked up to him and dropped to his knees." He rolled his eyes as he grinned widely at him. "Sorry, buddy, but it's true." With a shrug, Tyler added, "I've seen you get hit on in bars by guys, and you've been completely oblivious to it."

"Really?" Brett had no idea what Tyler was talking about. "Huh."

Brett had never really thought about being with a guy before. He didn't have a problem with it, per se, but it was always so easy for him to pick up women. Even when Brett had noticed that a guy was attractive, he'd never seen a reason to try to go that route.

"Well, Brett isn't a fag," Karissa stated derisively with an eye-roll. She lifted her chin and smiled. "So he's out of luck."

"Watch your mouth," Trina snapped, frowning at the other woman. "My brother's gay, and I don't like that term."

"Whatever," Karissa muttered with another eye-roll.

Preall eyed Brett, and he wondered what the older man was looking for. "Well, let me and Trina set up camp. Then we'll take a look at the map and decide where to go." Sliding his arm back around Trina's waist, he turned and headed toward their campsite.

As Brett allowed Karissa to urge him toward their own space, he wondered what the others had obviously seen that he'd completely missed.

And why do I care if Nedrick's interested? That doesn't really matter to me.

Does it?

CHAPTER THREE

Driving away from his mate while he was in the clutches of that hussy was the hardest thing Nedrick had ever had to do in his life. He gripped the steering wheel tightly as he drove along the winding roads toward town. Nedrick focused on his breathing, while reminding his wolf that they would see their mate again . . . soon.

Preall will let me know where to meet them. It won't be long before we see our mate again.

With that silent promise made to the snarling wolf he shared his psyche with, Nedrick focused on his driving. The trek to Stone Ridge was short, and he drove through the open gate to the left of Kade's mechanic's shop. A quick glance showed him that the car dolly was right where he thought it would be.

As Nedrick backed his *Jeep* up to it, he spotted Kade as he exited the back of the shop and began striding toward him. He was a little surprised to see the wolf shifter enforcer there on a Saturday. The man usually reserved the weekends for pack business and time with his human mate, Tom.

After parking his vehicle in front of the dolly, Nedrick cut the engine. He hopped out, as did Rierdon, who'd been sitting quietly in the passenger seat. Nedrick had appreciated that his buddy hadn't tried to discuss the situation with him. In truth, it had taken all of Nedrick's self-control to keep his agitated wolf in check while driving.

"Hi, Ned," Kade greeted with a smile as he glanced between them. "What's up?"

Before Nedrick could explain, Rierdon blurted, "My truck broke down at Tall Timbers Campground. Ned came to help me, and he found his mate there." Hardly taking a breath, he rambled, "Is there someone here that can help me instead, so Ned can go back and woo his mate? He's up there camping with a redheaded hussy named Karissa."

Kade's jaw sagged open for an instant, and his dark eyebrows shot up as his eyes widened. "Say what now?" A second later, he shook his head once, as if clearing it, and lifted his hand, obviously asking for Rierdon to keep silent. Then he turned his attention to Nedrick. "You found your mate, Ned?"

Nedrick nodded. "Yeah. He's a human camping with a group of friends for the week."

"Congratulations," Kade rumbled, grabbing Nedrick in a quick hug. After a pat on the back, he stepped back and returned his attention to Rierdon. "What's this about a hussy named Karissa?"

Clenching his jaw, Nedrick blew out a sharp breath through his nostrils. He fought the urge to growl, and he felt a muscle begin ticking in his jaw. Fortunately, Rierdon answered for him again.

"Yeah, total skank-city." Rierdon crossed his arms and scowled while staring at the car dolly. "She kept pressing her boobs against him and grabbing his arm possessively." Curling his lip, Rierdon grumbled, "Ugh, and the way she carded her fingers through his hair almost made *me* want to yank her away from him." Shaking his head, he focused on Nedrick. "I don't know how you kept your cool, Ned."

Letting out the rumbling growl, Nedrick recalled each scene Rierdon painted. He couldn't remember the last time he'd lost control of his wolf, even a little, once Alpha Declan had taught him how to balance his urges. Right then, however, Nedrick felt his skin begin to tingle as his hair threatened to change to fur, and his fingertips began to ache with the impending growth of his claws.

"Calm down, Nedrick," Kade ordered, pressing close to him. "Breathe in my scent." He wrapped one hand tightly around Nedrick's torso in a bear hug while threading his fingers into Nedrick's hair and urging him to tuck his face against his neck. "Take solace in the scent of your pack," Kade rumbled, soft and low. "Your enforcer's got your back."

Nedrick obeyed, inhaling the familiar scent of wolf and pack—his family. Resting his hands loosely on Kade's waist, he stood like that for a moment and just breathed. He slowly reined in his wolf's jealousy . . . and his own, and regained control of himself.

"Shit, Ned," Rierdon murmured, worry and concern filling his tone. "I'm so sorry. That was so stupid of me."

"Is'okay," Nedrick mumbled, glancing up to meet Rierdon's pale features and offering him a tight smile. Then he took several more calming breaths before lowering his hands and raising his head. "Guess I was more on edge than I realized."

Kade's deep brown-eyed gaze bored into Nedrick's for a heartbeat, two. "You okay?" he asked quietly.

Nedrick nodded slowly. "Yeah. Much better." When Kade's grip eased, he took a step backward while shaking his head. "Damn."

"Yeah, damn." Kade scoffed softly, shoving his hands into the front pockets of his jeans. "Finding your mate while he's dating someone else is . . . intense."

Grimacing, Nedrick nodded. He recalled how Kade had found his own human mate in a similar situation. The enforcer had shown up at a restaurant to act as the fourth in a double date as a favor to his adopted sister for two reasons— so she wouldn't be a third wheel and to vet the guy her friend was dating. As it turned out, the man Kade was supposed to vet was his mate.

"Except, you didn't start to lose your shit," Nedrick grumbled, frowning. "Not that I heard anyway."

Kade shrugged. "I didn't have to witness any behavior like Rierdon described from the date, either." Then he clapped his hands together and rubbed them together as his expression turned feral. "So, who's your mate? And did you at least get his phone number?"

"His name's Brett Robinson, and no, I didn't get his phone number," Nedrick admitted. Seeing Kade's expression turn speculative, he quickly added, "But he's friends with Preall and Trina. Preall's going to let me know where they're going hiking."

"So you can crash it," Kade guessed with a knowing nod. "Good. And friends with a fellow shifter. Excellent." Rubbing his goateed chin, Kade speculated, "And you said he's here for the week, so we'll put a plan in place to get him away from this Karissa hussy so you have a chance to seduce him and steal him away from her." Peering intently at him, Kade asked, "Got any read on how long they've been together? You know the mate-pull will help in your favor." He pulled out his phone and woke the device. "I'll text Preall and see if he can give us information on your Brett."

"Not a clue, so I'd appreciate that," Nedrick admitted, but then he couldn't help curving his lips into a shit-eating grin. "But I've already taken some of his blood, so even if Brett doesn't understand why, he's gonna be drawn to me and start feeling uncomfortable with her touch."

Kade barked a laugh as he snapped his focus back to Nedrick. "Well, damn, Ned. Nice one." His dark eyes twinkled with mischief. "How'd you manage that?"

With his grin firmly in place, Nedrick explained about Karissa startling Brett into dropping the tire and the subsequent cut on his finger. He'd realized pretty darn quick that Brett wasn't good with blood. Acting on his instinct to soothe his mate came naturally, and Nedrick hadn't even tried to stay his reaction to lick away the scary liquid, mostly seal the wound, and to take away his pain.

The fact that Nedrick felt his wolf rumble happily in his mind as he felt the beginnings of their bond was a very pleasant side-effect.

Chuckling, Kade nodded. "Okay, well, you've already got one foot in the door, then, so to speak." He patted Nedrick on the shoulder. "Well done."

Another thought occurred to Nedrick, and he found his smile fading as worry replaced the pleasure of his enforcer's praise. "You don't think he's going to feel manipulated when he finds out." He rubbed the back of his neck and squinted at Kade. "Do you?"

Shrugging his wide, thickly muscled shoulders, Kade offered, "Even if Brett does, he'll get over it." He smiled encouragingly. "It's the way of paranormals. In time, he'll come to understand."

"I hope so," Nedrick responded quietly.

Kade's phone dinged, and he read what was on the screen. The corners of his lips quirked up. He turned his phone around so Nedrick could read the screen. Kade had received a text from Preall.

Tyler tells me Brett and Karissa have only been dating a couple of weeks. She seems far more vested than him. He's never dated a guy, though, and he had no clue Ned was into him. Tyler says he's really oblivious about that kind of thing. LOL.

"Huh," Nedrick murmured. "So he wasn't just ignoring my touches." With a low chuckle, he claimed, "Guess I'll have to step up my game and be more overt."

"Sounds like it," Kade confirmed.

Just then, Nedrick's phone chimed, and he discovered his own text from Preall.

We're heading to Lake Donita Flats for a picnic. Tabatha and Karissa wanted to start off with an easy hike. I'm sure you won't have any trouble catching up to us.

Nedrick quickly responded with his thanks, confirming that he would see them there.

Just as Nedrick hit send, another message from Preall popped up on the screen.

Fair warning. Karissa knows you're after her guy, and I think she's more than a little homophobic. Trina's brother, mate, and a couple of the other guys are meeting us, too, so it could get interesting.

Feeling his eyes widen, Nedrick flipped his phone around so Kade and Rierdon could read Preall's warning.

Kade scoffed as he shook his head.

Rierdon wrinkled his nose. "Yeah, I got that vibe off her."

"Well, at least you'll have plenty of backup if Jason and Michel and their crew are joining you." Kade gripped Nedrick's shoulder and squeezed lightly. "Keep me posted on how it's going, okay? And I'll give Alpha and Beta a heads up about the situation."

"Yes, sir," Nedrick replied automatically to the stronger wolf. "Thank you."

Nedrick knew that Jason was Trina's older brother and a very out and proud gay man. Michel was a wolf shifter only a couple of decades shy of four hundred years. He was big, grizzled, and didn't take shit from anyone. If Karissa made the mistake of saying something homophobic to Jason, woman or not, Michel would put her in her place.

There were several other mated couples in their tight-knit circle of friends, so it would be interesting to see who turned up to hike. They were all fated pairs, and with a number of them, one look was all a person needed to peg them as gay. Any comments toward any of them wouldn't be received well.

Not at all. This may be a train wreck in the making.

Kade nodded once before looking at Nedrick's *Jeep*, then at Rierdon. "And I'll get Baker to go get your truck, Rierdon." He slung his arm over the smaller shifter's shoulders and began guiding him toward the shop. "Your shifts will be covered for the foreseeable future while we help you figure this out, Ned, so get out of here," he called over his shoulder. Peering back at him, Kade winked. "And good luck."

"Thanks."

Needing no further encouragement, Nedrick hopped back behind the wheel of his *Jeep* and headed toward Lake Donita Flats trailhead.

Chapter Four

Spotting the sign for Lake Donita Flats trailhead, Brett barely held in his sigh of relief. He couldn't help how uncomfortable Karissa's continued possessiveness was plaguing him. He enjoyed a pair of boobs pressed against his side as well as the next man, but she was being ridiculous.

Somehow, Karissa had, during the drive, managed to lean across the gap between their front chairs and touch him . . . *a lot*. Considering his prick was not interested . . . at all . . . the contact was making him feel more than a little uneasy. She was a very pretty woman. He'd always thought so, but she was acting way over the top, in his opinion.

Once Brett had parked, he was more than happy to jump out of his *GMC*. It allowed him to extricate himself from Karissa's sudden clingy-vine-ness. He watched her hop out, too, and move around the front toward him, so he headed toward the back and popped the back hatch.

Brett noticed Tyler exiting from the backseat behind him, a smirk on his good-looking features. He could see the mirth in his best friend's green eyes. His buddy was getting a kick out of Brett's discomfort, which he knew his long-time friend was able to see in him.

Asshole.

Fortunately, Tyler exiting the *Envoy* made Karissa detour a little, giving him a little extra time.

Just give me a few goddammed minutes without her trying to rub against me like a bitch-cat in heat.

By the time Karissa reached him, Brett had located her

27

shoulder bag and picked it up. He did his best to smile as he held it out to her. "Here ya go, K." After she'd taken it on instinct, Brett returned his attention to the other peoples' supplies that had been tossed into his vehicle and began pulling things out. "Okay," he muttered, doing his best to ignore Karissa's hovering. "Who else needs what?"

To his relief, Brett really didn't need an answer as Tyler slipped between him and Karissa and began grabbing his and Tabatha's stuff from the back. He took a step backward, watching. Brett felt Karissa grab his arm again, having slipped between the other couple, and he just managed to keep from rolling his eyes.

As gently as he could, Brett extricated himself. "Gotta get my own bag," he explained as he moved toward his *Envoy*.

Before more could be said, Brett heard the low rumbles of motorcycle engines. He'd thought about getting one once or twice, but there was no way that he could afford even a half-way-decent one without getting into debt. There really was no way to justify racking up that expense while he was a starving college student.

Brett turned his attention toward the other side of the parking lot and watched three bikes of varying styles and ages glide into the lot. Each had a pair of men on them. Pretty large men drove two of them with much smaller guys on the back. The third was driven by a huskily muscular-looking male with a slightly taller, slenderer guy behind him. All the machines, while older models, appeared to be in great shape.

Nice lookin' grouping.

Almost as one, the bikers parked. The guys on the backs hopped off, and the men in front followed suit.

As Brett watched, the driver with the thick, gray-threaded beard removed his helmet, then his passenger's, setting them on the motorcycle's seat. He dropped to one knee before the small man who'd ridden behind him. He unbuckled the much younger guy's chaps, then reached down and unzipped them halfway up his calves. Finally, with the smaller man's hands on the large man's shoulders, he helped him step out of them, revealing the shortest jean shorts Brett had ever seen on a man.

While the pair had an obvious age difference, they were clearly *not* a father-son pair. That became obvious when the bearded biker rested his hand on the other man's calf. He skimmed his hand up the back of the guy's knee . . . and thigh . . . only to palm the younger man's pert derrière. It was even obvious from the flex of the biker's thumb that he was giving it a squeeze.

Obviously not shy, the man laughed while grinning down at his . . . partner. His green eyes were filled with heat, and a second later, he bent and pecked a kiss to the bearded man's lips. That drew a smile and softening of the big man's hard features.

Brett thought it was actually kind of . . . unexpectedly sweet.

"Jason!" Trina cried, skipping across the gravel lot toward the pair, her arms held wide in the air. "You're here!"

The smaller man—Jason—turned and opened his own arms in welcome, a huge grin on his pretty features. "Trina!"

As the pair crashed together—Jason grabbing Trina around the waist and spinning her around, laughing happily—the bearded man took a few steps back. Obviously, he'd been expecting the display and was ready to offer them room. Preall also closed the gap and held out his hand to the older man who'd been driving the large *Harley.*

"Good to see you, Michel," Preall greeted.

Michel grabbed Preall's hand and tucked him into a one-armed bro-hug with plenty of back-slaps.

"Good to see ye, too," Michel rumbled, his voice gravelly and rough with a hint of an Irish lilt. "Been missin' ye, but I understand why." The big man cut a glance toward where Jason and Trina were still gabbin' and gossipin'.

"Won't always be like this," Preall replied with a wide smile. Then he headed over to the pair and pulled them both into a big hug. "Jason! So good to see ya."

The slender auburn-haired male laughed and hugged him back. "You, too, man." Easing away, he tried to affect a stern look that only looked cute on his pretty features. "You takin' good care of my sister, man?"

Trina hip-checked Jason as she rolled her eyes and puhshawed. "Of course, he is." Then she grabbed Jason's hand and urged him toward Brett's group. "Come meet my friends."

Jason grinned and tugged her back. "Just a sec." He turned back to Michel. "Be right back, Mich," he told him. Then he pecked a kiss to Michel's lips again before following Trina's lead.

"Ugh, more faggots," Karissa mumbled, soft and low.

Brett barely resisted scowling.

What the hell?

This is Tabatha's friend from years back?

"Hey. Shut it," Tabatha hissed, having obviously heard her. "You knew coming up here that Trina's brother was gay."

"Didn't think I'd have their depravity shoved in my face," Karissa softly snarled back. "Why are you—"

Brett tuned out the rest of that conversation when he saw five sets of eyes focus in their direction—Preall, Jason's big guy, Michel, the two guys that had been on a second bike, and the blond-haired driver of the third bike. The last man—another cute blond who'd shed his chaps to reveal equally tiny jean shorts—touched the arm of the blond who'd driven their bike and received a whispered comment, which made the guy narrow his eyes. They were all staring at Karissa.

If Brett hadn't known better, he would've sworn they'd

overheard her homophobic comments, even from halfway across the parking lot.

So glad I haven't banged her.

Maybe this'll help me explain to Tyler and Tabatha why I've lost interest. Her attitude leaves a lot to be desired.

After that, the image of the handsome-looking, sandy-blond-haired mechanic drifted across his thoughts. He pushed that away, too. He would have no idea what to do with a guy anyway.

But Ned would, right?

Brett fought the urge to shake his head as he watched the group of guys approaching. At the same time, Tabatha pulled Karissa toward the restroom. Maybe she was going to try to talk some sense into her friend, get her to calm down, be nice.

Hell, if I know.

Closing his GMC's rear door, Brett slung his backpack over one shoulder and waited beside Tyler. "So, Trina's brother's friends are gay bikers," Tyler mused.

Shrugging, Brett leaned against his vehicle's bumper and replied just as softly, "Guess so."

Before more could be said, the chimes of several cell phones going off filled the air. Almost as one, the six new arrivals pulled out their phones. The brows of several of them lifted in obvious surprise, and the blond pair exchanged looks. The shortest dark-haired man who'd been driving the middle bike smirked and scoffed before slinging his arm around the taller guy who'd ridden with him. Michel, however, his eyes narrowed.

All of them exchanged glances before showing each other their phones. Then they focused on Preall, and a couple of whispered comments ensued. Preall nodded once, glanced Brett's way, then smiled and shrugged.

Several snickers erupted, including from Trina, who was immediately pulled by Preall into his side. He dipped his head and whispered something. She blushed, and Brett wondered if he was chiding her for something.

What the hell is going on?

A ball of unease tightened in Brett's gut.

"Well, this'll be fun," Michel rumbled, starting toward him once more. Then, to Brett's surprise, Michel held out his hand to him and even offered a small smile. "Hi. Brett, is it?"

Brett nodded and took Michel's hand. "Yeah. Brett Robinson."

"Michel McDover." The guy squeezed but not hard enough to hurt—as if they were in a pissing contest. "Good to meet ye." Then he released Brett and held his hand out to Tyler and offered him the same greeting. After that, Michel turned, slipped his arm around Jason's waist, and pulled him close to his side. "This is me partner, Jason. I gather ye already know he's Trina's brother."

Tyler chuckled. "A little hard to miss, man."

Nodding, Michel indicated the rest of the group. "That's Luther with his partner Deke." He pointed at the pair of blonds. After that, he pointed at the darker-haired couple. "And that's Jamie and Paolo."

Just as Michel was finishing up introductions, the girls returned from the two-door unisex brick bathroom. Introductions ensued once more. At least that gave Brett the opportunity to affix everyone's name to their faces. He'd always had a little trouble with that.

"Jamie and I'll wait for Nedrick," Paolo claimed, slipping his arm around the slightly taller slenderer Jamie. "You guys go ahead." He eyed Karissa's perfectly new, clean, and pristine, hiking boots critically. "I'm sure we won't have any trouble catching up."

Paolo obviously didn't have much faith in Karissa's athletic ability. Brett couldn't say that he blamed him. She'd been the one to insist on an easy hike to a secluded picnic-friendly location.

Fortunately, Preall had known how to fulfill her request.

"You don't mind?" Paolo cupped Jamie's jaw as he turned and peered up at him. "Do you, baby?"

"Never mind hangin' with you, P," Jamie crooned back.

Paolo hummed before urging Jamie to dip his head. He pressed a lingering kiss to the slightly taller man's lips, and it almost seemed as if Jamie sank into the shorter, thicker man. Paolo must have taken that as permission to take the kiss deeper, for he notched their faces more fully and did just that.

There were a number of chuckles, as well as ribbings of, *get a room.* Even a couple of wolf whistles rent the air. Those almost drowned out Karissa's muttered hiss of, *disgusting.*

While Tabatha nudged Karissa's arm and Michel narrowed his eyes a smidge while glancing her way, no one else commented. It also didn't stop the pair from their make-out session. When Preall laughed and urged the rest of them toward the trailhead, Brett wasn't certain if he was relieved or disappointed. With bags or backpacks on everyone's backs, the group — minus the making out pair — followed Preall's leave.

Watching the pair make-out was a little like watching porn. They were definitely making love to each other with their mouths. They clutched at each other, and Paolo had threaded his fingers into Jamie's hair in an obviously dominant move to control the kiss.

It was really quite . . . *hawt!*

Just . . . dayam!

"Come on," Karissa encouraged, reaching for Brett's hand. "Let's get in front of everyone."

Before Karissa could drag him forward, Luther slipped between them, stopping her from grabbing him. "Sorry about that," he commented, absently glancing Karissa's way, before focusing on him. "So, Brett, Trina says you're going into your senior year of college, same as her. What are you studying?"

Appreciating Luther's move, Brett did his best to ignore Karissa's annoyed expression. "Uh, I'm getting a degree in engineering," he told him.

"Yeah?" Luther peered at him with an interested expression. "What do you want to focus on? Houses? Boats? Bridges?" His grin appeared friendly. "What's your passion?"

"Houses, actually," Brett admitted. "I love housing design." After a second of hesitation, he shared, "Especially smaller wood-framed structures." Indicating the woods around them, which were beautiful, Brett told him, "It's why I really wanted to get up here and explore. There are so many different styles of homes up here in the woods."

"That there are," Luther agreed. Narrowing his eyes, he asked, "Do you know how to ride a motorcycle? It's the best way to explore these winding roads."

Brett shook his head. "Uh, no." With a deprecating laugh, he told him, "Have looked at them. Even picked up the motorcycle license requirement handbook from the DMV." Shaking his head, Brett admitted, "Never got that far though."

"Well, no problem." Luther patted him on the back. "Ned has a motorcycle. A lot of the guys around here do." Grinning, he continued, "You can ride with him. We'll find time to show you the sights while you're here."

Before Brett could respond in favor of that plan—it seemed these guys sure didn't have a problem with other guys riding bitch—Karissa ducked around Luther and grabbed his hand. "We'll be too busy," she declared. Turning away from Luther—who looked surprisingly amused by her rudeness—Karissa hurried Brett forward. "Come on, sweetie. Let's go."

With Karissa's grip so tight, Brett fought back a wince and let her have her way.

Good grief.

CHAPTER FIVE

When Nedrick arrived at the trailhead, he spotted several motorcycles, Brett's *Envoy*, and Preall's SUV. He also noticed Paolo and Jamie lounging on the grass in the shade near the motorcycles. After parking, Nedrick leaped from his *Jeep* and headed toward them.

The guys were on their feet instantly, moving toward him, too. While Paolo appeared as amused as hell, Jamie's expression screamed of concern. Then the very dominant rat shifter tugged the submissive wolf shifter against his side, holding him close, and Jamie practically sagged into his mate as they came to a stop.

"Hey, Ned." Paolo grinned up at him. "Congratulations, man."

While Paolo's shorter stature of five-foot-seven didn't seem like much, he had broad shoulders and thick muscles. His attitude also screamed dominant. The guy considered caring for his mate, a more reserved five-foot-nine wolf shifter, of the utmost importance.

As it should be.

"Hi, Paolo," Nedrick greeted. "Jamie." After glancing between them and getting a sweet smile from the small wolf shifter, he peered toward the trailhead. "I'm guessing they're already on their way."

"Yep," Paolo agreed amicably, turning in that direction. "Jamie, love." He pecked a kiss to his mate's cheek. "Grab our backpacks with our picnic shit. Would you please?"

"Yes, sir," Jamie immediately responded before bounding

toward the motorcycles.

Paolo started strolling toward the trailhead slowly, obviously giving his mate time to grab their stuff, and Nedrick fell into step beside him. "You're right," Paolo offered as they walked, shaking his head. "That Karissa is a piece of work. Homophobic with a possessive streak a mile wide." Paolo's grin turned maniacal as he cackled a little. "But don't worry. The guys and I got your back." With a wink, he turned around and started walking backward so he could keep an eye on his mate. "We're already paving the way for getting Brett used to the idea of men together while showcasing just how bitchy his date is."

Nedrick wondered just what Paolo meant by that, but he held his tongue as a middle-aged man and woman dressed in outdoor apparel appeared around the bend before them. The pair smiled at them, and they exchanged greetings and *have a good hike* pleasantries. They'd just disappeared from sight when Jamie jogged up with a backpack slung over each shoulder. Paolo immediately took one of them and slipped it over his own back before giving the man a peck.

"Thanks, baby," Paolo crooned with a heated smile. Then he grabbed his lover's hand, threaded their fingers, and refocused on the hike. "So, we made out in front of everyone a little after agreeing to wait here for you."

Jamie snickered. "A little?" The wolf shifter smirked as he hip-checked Paolo. "That was more than a little, my mate."

"Indeed, it was," Paolo rumbled. With a leer at Jamie, he added, "And making out with you is never a hardship." Then he returned his attention to Nedrick and told him, "Karissa's definitely a bigot, just like Preall warned. We overheard some not-so-nice stuff she whispered."

Jamie lifted his free hand and tapped the side of his head. "Shifter hearing."

Nedrick nodded, understanding. Shifter hearing could easily pick up comments that humans had thought they'd whispered. Plus, considering his own interaction with her, he didn't think she was all that subtle. Hell, she'd probably barely even whispered.

Pushing those thoughts away, Nedrick glanced between the mated pair. "Anything else I should be ready for?"

Paolo shrugged. "Luther said he and Deke were going to try to engage your mate." He smirked and winked. "Do their best to try to keep his attention on them as opposed to Karissa. That sort of thing."

Nedrick nodded, contemplating that. Considering the self-centered, needy way she'd been acting at the campground, he could see how that would be effective. She was all about keeping Brett's attention on herself. Having to share him would piss her off.

Gods, I do love my pack.

"Perfect," Nedrick murmured. "Let's pick up the pace."

Paolo and Jamie laughed, but they were happy to oblige. When Nedrick broke into a jog, the other shifters easily kept up.

Nedrick heard the group before he spotted them. Having hiked the trail about a million times, he knew there was an arcing bend just before the meadow and stream came into view. He slowed down to a stroll and took a few deep, measured breaths.

All that did was allow him to pick up the lingering hints of Brett's unique and exotic scent.

His prick twitched as his blood heated.

Great.

Dismissing that, Nedrick paused, doing his best to ignore his wolf's urging to keep moving. He lifted his arms over his head and stretched. Then he bent at the waist and arched his back.

After straightening, Nedrick glanced at the pair with him. He rolled his eyes upon seeing their matching grins. With a shake of his head, he started forward again, making certain he kept at a leisurely pace.

"You got this, Ned," Jamie murmured encouragingly.

"You really do, man," Paolo seconded. "And we got your back."

Nedrick nodded, then slowly rounded the bend. After climbing another twenty feet of trail up a sharp slope, the meadow stretched out before him. There were spring wild-flowers in bloom everywhere, covering the area in shades of purples, blues, whites, and reds. Tufts of green grass sprouted up between them, creating a unique kaleidoscope of colors before him.

Two large blankets had been spread out, and everyone was sitting in a circle around them. Food and drink containers littered the fabric. Most of them held plates and chatted between taking bites.

Preall, Trina, Michel, and Jason were engaging Tyler and Tabatha along one side of the blanket. Luther and Deke sat opposite them, toward the right, and were talking with Brett. His mate was sitting on the edge of the blanket with a plate on his lap. Karissa sat between Tabatha and Brett, leaning close to him. Well, she was pressed against his side and probably wished she was on his lap, considering the way she literally held his arm around her waist and clutched their other hands together. Each time Brett wanted to take a bite of food, he had to tug his hand away from hers to do it. Then Karissa grabbed him again.

For an instant, Nedrick saw red.

How dare she touch what's mine!

"Settle, Ned," Paolo ordered, his voice low and strong. "Calm the fuck down." Even though the male was a rat shifter, he was a damn dominant one, and when Paolo stated, "You'll earn no points by rushing over and acting the fool,"

Nedrick found himself responding.

Taking a deep breath, Nedrick forced his gaze away from Brett and Karissa. He noticed the second Luther registered his presence. The wolf shifter snapped his attention Nedrick's way and appeared to be preparing to stand . . . as if he planned to stop him from doing something foolish.

Like rip out Karissa's throat.

Yeah, that wouldn't endear me to my mate.

Nedrick forced down his instinct to head straight to Brett. Instead, he kept his pace to a leisurely stroll toward Michel's end of the blanket. He knew the mere presence of the older, stronger wolf would help him settle his own animal.

When they were ten feet away, Michel focused on them, his gaze flicking between them. His bearded lips curved into a small smile, although the move didn't reach his eyes. He nodded toward the picnic food spread out on the blankets.

"Hey, guys." Michel's dark-eyed stare bore into Nedrick. "Have a seat. Grab some chow. Relax for a bit."

Nedrick and his wolf knew an order when they heard one. "Food sounds great right about now," he replied with a grin.

Considering there was a considerable gap between Deke and Jason . . . who was actually sitting on Michel's lap, Nedrick headed that way. Jamie settled next to Michel and Jason with Paolo by his side. Nedrick bent and took the paper plate offered to him by Jason and almost began to kneel.

Then Nedrick spotted the large container of turkey and cheese croissant sandwiches in front of Luther.

Perfect.

With an internal smirk, Nedrick moved toward his fellow wolf shifter. He placed his left foot between Luther and Brett and lowered his right knee to the ground behind his mate, subtly nudging his back with his leg. Nedrick rested his forearm on Brett's shoulder, grinning at his human when the man he wanted to touch and taste peered up at him in surprise.

"Did you enjoy your hike?" Nedrick asked Brett.

"Uhhh, y-yeah," Brett confirmed, nodding.

With Brett's attention focused on Nedrick, his mate probably missed Karissa's sneer as she looked at him. If looks could kill, Nedrick would have been writhing in pain. Fortunately, they couldn't.

"Glad to hear it," Nedrick replied affably, pressing his leg into Brett's side a little harder before easing off. "There's definitely many more gorgeous places around here. Can't wait to show them to you." Nedrick saw Karissa open her mouth, and he could just imagine what vitriol she was preparing to spout. Not giving her a chance, he turned his attention to Luther and indicated the container of turkey croissants with his plate. "Hold that up for me, would ya, Luth?"

Dutifully, Luther grabbed the large *Tupperware* and held it up. "Here ya go, Ned." Mischief danced in the shifter's blue eyes, and Nedrick knew the other shifter was aware of exactly what he was doing and seemed only too happy to play along. "Deke's homemade chipotle mayo is on there."

Rubbing his chest against Brett's upper arm as he reached forward to place two sandwiches on his plate, Nedrick groaned. "Oh, hell yeah, man. Thanks, Deke." He eased back and licked his lips as he eyed Luther's grinning mate. "I love your chipotle mayo, Deke. So damn good."

Deke's cheeks flushed as he grinned widely, clearly pleased by the compliment. "You're welcome. Glad you like it."

"More than like," Nedrick claimed. Waggling his brows at the man comically, he teased, "If I didn't know Luther would pull my spine out through my balls, I'd try to steal ya away."

Luther growled, but fortunately, there was no true anger in it, so Nedrick's wolf wasn't worried. "Get your own mate," he snapped, wrapping his arm around Deke.

Nedrick barked a laugh and nodded. "Workin' on it, Luth. Workin' on it." Then he turned his attention to a wide-eyed

Brett and winked. To his pleasure, Nedrick caught the slightest whiff of surprise, tinged with a hint of embarrassment and even arousal. *Yes! My mate's not immune to me.* Instead of calling attention to it, Nedrick pointed at a container of red *Jello* near Karissa's knee. "I'd love some of that, if you'll hold it up for me, Brett."

Brett blinked once, as if needing to regain his focus. "Uh, yeah." He looked toward where Nedrick had indicated. "Here."

In order to grab the dish and lift it toward him, Brett needed both hands. Not only did he remove his arm from around a clearly perturbed Karissa's waist, but he freed his second hand from her, too. Brett held it up, and Nedrick smiled his thanks as he used the large spoon to dish some onto his plate.

"Thanks, handsome," Nedrick stated with a smile. Then he squeezed Brett's shoulder, pretending to need the grip to rise back to his feet. "Oh, look at that. Crackers and salmon dip. Yum." Before moving away, Nedrick took the opportunity to slide his right hand up his mate's shoulder to his nape so he could tease his fingers through the man's thick auburn hair.

Pulling away was damn difficult, especially noticing the way his mate's arms goose bumped, but Nedrick did it. He headed toward the open space between Deke and Paolo. Settling Indian-style between them, he grabbed a plastic fork from the red solo cup in the middle of the blankets.

Nedrick ignored Karissa's hate-filled glare—which she quickly hid when Brett returned his attention to his plate—as well as Paolo's amused smirk, and he used the fork to point at the aforementioned salmon dip and crackers. "Can you pass that my way, man?" Then he scooped up a forkful of the *Jello*, pleased to see it contained slices of banana, chunks of pineapple, and grape halves.

"Sure." Paolo slid the requested items his way.

"What do you want to drink, Ned?" Preall asked, indicating a soft-sided cooler. "Beer, wine, soda, water?"

"I'll take a beer," Nedrick answered after swallowing the strawberry-flavored goodness.

Nedrick placed the fork on his plate and the plate on his knee. After taking the bottle, he popped the cap. While taking a drink, Nedrick cut a side-eye look toward his mate, pleased to see that Brett hadn't allowed Karissa to grab his hands again. Instead, his mate had picked up his plate with one hand and a fork with his other while he was eating potato salad.

Mmmm . . . that sounds good, too.

"I'm gonna go for a swim, Michel," Jason declared, drawing everyone's attention. He hopped off his big lover's lap before bending and pecking a kiss to Michel's lips. "Wanna come?"

"Always wanna come," Michel countered with a smirk as he lifted a hand and squeezed Jason's shorts-covered ass, making several people laugh, including Jason. "But I'll pass on the swimming for now. Go have fun."

Jason grinned broadly as he whipped his shirt over his head, and Michel stared avidly at his lean torso. When he toed off his shoes — a hiking variety that had five toes — he revealed toenails painted in pink and green. With another wink in Michel's direction, Jason sashayed toward the lake.

Over his shoulder, Jason called, "Coming, Deke?"

"Most definitely later," Deke replied as he bounced to his feet, leering at Luther. "But I'd enjoy a swim."

A round of good-natured groans mixed with chuckles filled the air. A couple of people threw napkins at Deke, who just laughed while removing his own shirt. Then he bent to peck a kiss to Luther's lips, but the blond wolf shifter cupped Deke's head and held him still so he could ravish him for a good ten seconds before releasing him.

With flushed cheeks, Deke purred, "Promises, promises."

Luther grinned. "And I always deliver on my promises."

"Can't wait," Deke responded breathily before bouncing his way across the field after his friend.

Taking a bite of a turkey croissant—*oh, gods, so good*— Nedrick kept a discreet eye on Brett, wondering how he'd take the interaction. To his pleasure, he didn't seem to be fazed at all by his friends' antics. In fact, with the way Brett's lips were curved up just a little and the amusement dancing in his gorgeous green eyes, Nedrick would bet that he was fighting back a laugh.

Karissa, however, appeared to be fuming, considering the way her cheeks were flushed, and disgust filled her green eyes. She looked like she wanted to say something so badly, but she kept her lips pinched shut.

"You have a pond at home, Mich, and I know you enjoy the water often," Preall stated, drawing attention. "It's a beautiful day. How come you aren't swimming with Jason?"

"Because I swim in the nude," Michel stated bluntly while grabbing another beer and popping the cap. "Didn't think you'd appreciate Trina seeing the bone I'd end up with for Jason."

Even as many of them chuckled, including Nedrick, he heard Karissa's outraged gasp.

"Oh my god!" Karissa snapped. "How can you all laugh at something so perverted?"

"Well, while I sure don't want to see it," Trina stated crisply, scowling at Karissa. "There's nothing wrong with being attracted to the one you love."

Karissa's face turned even darker, but she snapped her mouth shut.

Yep. Deliciously scandalized.

Gods, I love my pack.

Chapter Six

For the most part, Brett enjoyed the hike and picnic at the lake. The guys were rowdy and a little bawdy, but they were friendly and welcoming, too. Most of them did their best to include Brett and draw him into conversation.

Brett noticed they even tried to engage Karissa, too, not that it worked very well. She responded with clipped, often one-word answers. Her distaste for the men was on clear display. Any real conversation from Karissa was reserved for Tabatha and Tyler. Even Trina and Preall were beginning to be given the cold shoulder.

On the hike back, Brett did his best to keep her from clutching his arm or holding his hand, but she was damn persistent. He enjoyed talking with Luther about possible houses to drive by, and while he wasn't much for cooking, he found Deke's enthusiasm engaging. Jason and Trina's sibling teasing was also entertaining as hell as they tried to embarrass each other in front of their significant others.

When they reached the trailhead, Brett took advantage of the restroom building and hit the head. He sighed deeply as he relieved his bladder. After shaking off and tucking himself away, Brett eyed his forearm as he washed his hands, wondering if he would end up with bruises from Karissa's claws.

Claws. Ha. That's exactly what they feel like, too.

Shaking his head, Brett exited the small room. The bright afternoon light made him squint. He blinked quickly, trying to get his eyes adjusted to the change from the dim stall.

Brett barely made out the broad shadow before he

slammed right into it. Bouncing backward a step, he tried to keep his balance. Knowing there was a cinderblock wall to his left that hid the two doors from view, Brett rocked that way with his arm out to catch it.

"Woah, easy, Brett." Two strong hands wrapped around Brett's upper arms, helping him steady.

Recognizing Nedrick's mellow tenor, Brett relaxed in the other man's grip. His eyesight finally cooperated, and he peered at Nedrick. The man stood about the same height, but there seemed to be a wealth of strength in his wiry body.

"You okay?" Nedrick asked, worry filling his brown eyes. He squeezed Brett's left upper arm lightly while rubbing a palm up and down his right. "I didn't hurt you, did I?"

Brett quickly shook his head. "I'm good," he assured. Seeing the concern in Nedrick's eyes, he took a swift glance around before quietly asking, "Were you hittin' on me earlier, while changing the tire?"

Nedrick smiled. "Yeah."

"And at the lake?" Brett had been pretty darn sure when Nedrick had knelt next to him. Even he wasn't *that* oblivious. "Pretty sure you were then, too."

Nedrick's smile widened into a broad grin, and his brown eyes twinkled. "And hell yeah."

"Why?" Brett cocked his head. He didn't get it.

"Because I'm attracted to you, Brett," Nedrick replied. He raked his gaze over Brett's body in a way that even he couldn't miss. "You're handsome, sexy, and I want to know more about you."

"Hey, where's Brett?"

Wincing upon hearing Karissa's voice drift through the air, Brett sighed.

Nedrick chuckled softly. "Don't worry," he rumbled, leaning closer. Lowering his voice, he whispered, "Our time will come soon enough, handsome."

Then, to Brett's shock, Nedrick leaned in and pecked a kiss to his lips. The feel of his surprisingly soft lips were there and gone so fast that if Brett had blinked, he surely would have missed it. With a wink, Nedrick released him and headed into the stall that he'd just vacated.

Brett touched his fingertips to his lips in amazement.

Did that just happen?

Except, Brett knew that it had. He rubbed his palm over his belly as he turned and headed away from the building. His stomach felt as if a dozen butterflies flitted within, and he realized that he had a chubby . . . again.

Damn. That's weird.

Except, the man's lips hadn't felt anything like what Brett had thought a guy's mouth would . . . not that he'd thought about it often. As he strode back toward the waiting group, he wondered if that was just a fluke. The touch had been there and gone so fast.

Would it be different if the kiss had been more?

Then Karissa bounced up to his side and grabbed his arm again, and Brett figured there was no point in wondering. After this outing, he doubted Karissa would leave him alone long enough to find out.

This is going to be a long week.

As they hiked along, Brett knew Karissa was pissed at him. The prior evening, he'd once again refused to sleep with her in her tent. He just didn't see the point in leading her on. Once they returned to campus, Brett hoped to never see her again except in passing when hanging out with Tyler and Tabatha.

Glad to see her true colors before anything went any further.

The hike they'd chosen today was quite a bit more difficult than yesterday's stroll. They were working their way through a forest with some pretty steep inclines. The group was minus Paolo and Jamie, as Paolo had to work. He was a firefighter, Brett found out. Instead, they'd been joined by Luther's cousin, Leopold—*just call me Leo*—as well as Leo's partner, Jerry. While Leo was a friendly guy with a ready grin, Jerry seemed quite reserved while cute, and his shy smile was achingly sweet.

Of course, Karissa had made another under-the-breath comment about *another couple of fags*.

With the way Luther and Leo had scowled at her, even though she'd been a good twenty feet away, Brett felt certain that they'd heard her. Leo had kept Jerry away from Brett unless Karissa was up the trail farther, chatting with Tabatha. It was during one of those times that Brett learned Jerry owned and operated a horse stable.

"Do you rent horses?" Brett asked. "I haven't been on a horse in years."

"We do," Jerry replied with a shy smile. "We even offer guided trail rides. Maybe you and your friends"—his attention flickered ahead to Karissa before returning to Brett—"well, *some* of your friends would like to see the mountains on horseback instead of hiking."

Brett understood the small man's concern. He'd obviously picked up on Karissa's rather toxic vibe, too.

Nodding, Brett told Jerry, "Hell, even if it's just me, I'd be interested in at least getting on one in an arena."

"You know Ned would go with you," Leo stated with a grin. "He'd be happy to—"

As if she realized someone was talking to Brett about Nedrick, Karissa cut off her conversation with Tabatha to stop and wait for Brett to catch up. Her green eyes were narrowed just a smidge as she eyed them. As soon as she was close enough, she took Brett's hand again.

"Watcha talkin' about?" Karissa asked.

"Horseback riding," Brett answered honestly.

"Ugg, why'd you want to go near those smelly animals?" Karissa turned her nose up as if she could smell something nasty right that second. "They're big, dumb, and dangerous."

Forcing a smile, Brett told Jerry, "I'll grab your number and talk to you about it later."

"Sounds good."

Leo was the one who replied. Then he used his hold on Jerry's hand to slow them both, falling into step near Luther and Deke.

"No, really?" Karissa demanded, scowling at him. "Why were you talking about horses with that fag?"

"Damn it, Karissa," Brett snapped, unable to help himself as his neck began to heat from embarrassment. "Watch your damn mouth already."

Karissa rolled her eyes. "Whatever."

At least she shut up.

A moment later, Preall called from near the front of the group. "We'll stop and rest just up ahead for a few minutes. There's a great view to enjoy."

"Good," Karissa huffed, a whine filling her tone. "I could use a break, and my feet are starting to hurt."

Brett wasn't certain who behind them said it, but he wasn't the only one who heard a guy say, "That's what you get for hiking for long periods in boots that aren't properly broken in."

Karissa scowled over her shoulder for a few seconds before snarling, "Whatever."

Just as Preall had promised, when they reached the plateau, the trees thinned to reveal an expansive clearing with a great view. Brett was impressed. They'd climbed much higher than he thought they had. The thick trees had hidden just how far up they were.

Standing with the others, Brett breathed in the fresh mountain air as he enjoyed the panoramic scene. He surveyed valleys and ridges of trees as far as the eye could see. There were even a few spots of blue, telling him where rivers ran.

"Gorgeous," Brett murmured, taking it all in.

"Why thank you," Karissa purred into his ear. "I think you're pretty hot yourself."

Brett barely refrained from doing his own eye-roll.

As Brett stood there, he felt his bladder twinge. He glanced around, wondering if he could step away and find a handy tree or bush. Spotting a likely clump of smaller evergreens, Brett started that way . . . with Karissa following, of course.

Once Brett had nearly reached his intended target, he tried to extricate himself from her hold. "Let go for a sec."

Karissa gripped his arm tighter. "Why? Where are you going?"

Pausing, Brett pointed at the cluster. "I'm going to step behind a tree and take a piss."

"Fine." Karissa curled her lip in disgust as she grumbled, "But don't be long. I don't wanna be stuck with all these fags by myself. Hurry up."

While Brett figured he shouldn't have been so blunt, he wasn't prepared for Karissa's sharp shove. He stumbled sideways a few steps and between a couple of bushes, their brambles catching the skin of his calves. Brett hissed and moved a few more steps without looking where he was going, and the earth fell away from beneath his feet.

With a sharp yell of surprise, Brett felt himself falling. That lasted only a couple of feet, and he landed on his ass. The momentum kept him moving, though, and he slid who knew how long until the ground gave way again.

Brett tried to grab onto a branch, but it broke. Careening down a sharper embankment, he flailed, trying to catch himself, only to slam his left arm against a set of jagged rocks. Pain erupted through his limb, and he instinctively tucked it close just as his feet hit soft dirt. The soil didn't hold his weight, and Brett barked another cry as he found himself tumbling into darkness.

When Brett finally stopped moving, he lay still in stunned silence on the earthen floor. He breathed slowly, trying to get his racing pulse to slow. Once he felt ready, Brett slowly eased into a sitting position, tucking his left arm to his chest, doing his best to ignore the pulsing ache radiating through it. All that did was make Brett aware of the myriad of other painful cuts and abrasions riddling his body.

Bowing his head, Brett focused on just calming himself. Slowly, he moved the rest of his limbs, and relief flooded him when he found everything else seemed in working order. After a few moments, Brett realized he heard the sound of several people shouting his name.

Relief filled him. Right. I'm not out here alone.

Even though his head was spinning, making his stomach twist uncomfortably, Brett tipped his chin up and hollered back. "I'm here." He rubbed his temple with his right hand for a couple of heartbeats before adding, "I'm in a hole."

A second later, Brett squinted up at the light filtering through said hole and made out the shape of someone's head and torso. He lifted his good hand. "Here."

Immediately, the torso turned into a lithe body as someone dropped into the cave with him. He landed in a crouch, making it look so easy. Then he straightened and rushed to Brett's side.

"Brett, baby," Nedrick cried, dropping to his knees beside him. He held his hands up as if he wanted to grab him, but he hesitated, clearly uncertain where to touch him. "Are you injured? Where's it hurt?"

"Guess I look about as bad as I feel," Brett muttered, offering a wry smile.

Nedrick frowned, sweeping his gaze over him again. His attention snagged on how he was holding his left arm. "Broke, you think?" Nedrick pointed at it.

"Yep, pretty sure," Brett confirmed, grimacing. "Can't use it, but I can wiggle my fingers. Sorta feels like when I broke my leg playing football in high school."

Grimacing, Nedrick nodded. "Then you won't be able to climb out yourself." Resting his left hand lightly on Brett's knee, he gently cradled Brett's jaw with his right. Nedrick peered deep into his eyes. "Did you hit your head? Think you have a concussion?"

Brett hummed. "Got a hell of a headache, so probably."

"Okay." Nedrick leaned forward and kissed his temple. "Don't worry. We'll have you out of here in no time."

Nedrick didn't seem to need a reply, for which Brett was grateful. His mouth was suddenly dry, and he felt the unmistakable urge to puke. Grimacing, Brett did his best to fight it.

Jumping to his feet, Nedrick moved to stand beneath the opening. That was when Brett noticed another person peering down at them.

"We're going to need a rope with a plank for Brett to sit on while we haul him up," Nedrick told him. "He's broken his wrist. Can one of the guys run down the trail until he gets service and call Lark?"

"Will do." Brett recognized Preall's voice. "I'll send Leo. He's fast. It might take us a bit of time to get enough rope or vines to fashion a sling for him, though."

"Thanks, man, and I get it," Nedrick replied. "Will you toss down the first aid kit and a pack with some water and trail mix or jerky or something?"

"Will do." Preall pulled away and said something to someone else, but Brett couldn't make it out. A second later, he reappeared, holding something over the opening. "Heads up."

A second later, Nedrick caught whatever Preall dropped. He set it aside, and Brett recognized the white cross on the large red bag. Nedrick caught something else, then turned and headed toward him. After placing the backpack on the ground, he returned to get the first aid kit.

"Sit tight, guys," Preall told him. "We'll have you out as

soon as possible." After a second, he added, "If you need anything, Michel will be close enough to hear you holler while the rest of us search."

"Thanks, Preall," Nedrick called before returning to Brett's side. "Damn, you're pale," he murmured, kneeling beside him. "Let's get ya a sip of water." He grabbed the backpack and opened it, pulling out a water bottle. After cracking the seal, instead of handing it to him, Nedrick cradled the back of Brett's head and held the bottle to his lips. "Just a little now."

Brett didn't fight him and took a small sip, then a second one. Even as he appreciated the cool, refreshing liquid sliding down his throat, he felt his bladder twinge. He grimaced as discomfort of a different nature flooded him.

"What is it?" Nedrick asked quickly, perhaps spotting his wince. "What's wrong?"

Nedrick rubbed his thumb over the skin under Brett's ear, sending tingles across his skin. They trickled south, which just confused his dick as he started to plump in his shorts. The sensation of unexpected arousal warred with his bladder's need for relief.

"Brett?" Nedrick urged.

"Well, I was heading into the trees to take a piss when Karissa pushed me," Brett explained, finding his tongue. Feeling his cheeks start to heat with embarrassment, he admitted, "Um, and I really still need to go."

"Karissa pushed you?" Nedrick growled, his eyes narrowing with anger flashing within them. "I'm gonna wring her—"

"Hey, uh, let's not, huh?" Brett quickly cut in. "Just let it go." Shifting his weight, he glanced toward the wall and judged the distance. Maybe he could slide to it and use it to stand. "Just gotta—"

Nedrick's eyes widened a second before he nodded. "Right, right." He swept his gaze over him. "I'm sure you'd rather stand to do that. Let me help you to your feet."

As Nedrick wrapped his arm around Brett's upper back and helped him to his feet, he felt his bladder clench again. While he wasn't a religious man, he prayed to whatever deity who might be listening that he wouldn't embarrass himself.

CHAPTER SEVEN

Nedrick helped Brett to his feet. While he relished the op-portunity to have his mate in his arms, he damn sure didn't like how it had come about. Still, his human's strong frame felt amazing pressed close against him.

Feeling Brett sway on his feet, Nedrick tightened his left arm around his waist while gripping his right upper arm. "Easy, there," he encouraged. "Take your time. Don't want you to fall."

"Really gotta piss," Brett countered through gritted teeth.

Wincing, Nedrick knew that feeling. Nature was calling to his sexy human.

Nodding, Nedrick carefully helped Brett turn to face the cave wall. "All right." He glanced toward his mate's fly before squeezing his upper arm. "Think you can manage one-handed?"

"Yeah." Brett placed his right hand on his fly and popped the button but hesitated on the zip. "You gonna watch?" he asked, arching a brow at him.

Nedrick barely resisted smirking at the man he soon hoped to make his lover. "Well, I'll look away if you're shy," he teased with a wink. Sobering, he added, "But I'm afraid you'll fall down if I release you, so, uh, yeah. Not going anywhere."

Brett frowned, pinching his lips in obvious indecision.

Hoping to help ease Brett's sudden bout of shyness, Nedrick took a step to the left and behind the other man. "I'll stand here behind you," he told him. Squeezing where he held his mate's waist and upper arm, he encouraged, "Do what you need to do, handsome."

With a sigh, Brett must have decided to just go with it.

Nedrick heard the telltale sound of a zipper being undone. Then his mate's shorts shifted beneath Nedrick's left hand, so he eased it higher up his waist. When his palm settled over the smooth, warm flesh of Brett's waist, just under the hem of his t-shirt, the hairs on Nedrick's arm stood on end, and he couldn't help rubbing his thumb along the flesh of his mate's back.

So good. So hard yet smooth.

Wonder if my mate feels like that everywhere.

The sound of urine hitting the dirt wall dragged Nedrick out of his lustful thoughts.

Right. Help my mate, then worry about seducing him.

Hearing Brett's soft moan of obvious relief caused Nedrick's lips to quirk up. He knew the feeling—one of relief mixed with pleasure. Sometimes, when your bladder was overly full, it just felt *really* good to pee.

Finally, the sound of Brett urinating tapered off before disappearing altogether. Nedrick felt it when his mate shook off, then seemed to lose his balance. When Brett took a shuffling step forward to catch himself, Nedrick pressed closer and wrapped his arms around his mate's torso to help.

"Easy, handsome," Nedrick crooned as Brett caught his balance. "No vigorous movements."

Brett sighed softly and shook his head once, slowly. "My head's ringing a bit," he admitted. He peered over his shoulder at him, revealing flushed cheeks. "Thanks for not letting me take a header into the wall I just pissed on."

Nedrick chuckled. "My pleasure." It was, too, because his left hand had slid farther up under Brett's shirt, and now he currently palmed his mate's hot, hard abdominals. "Go to the gym much?" Nedrick asked curiously, teasing his fingers along the grooves of Brett's stomach. His mate didn't have a full six-pack, but there was definite delineation there.

"Yeah," Brett mumbled, as he began righting his shorts. His voice dropped, taking on a note of huskiness. "Great stress relief from studying."

"I imagine so," Nedrick murmured, wondering when he would be able to get an eyeful of the flesh he felt under his hands. While his right hand cradled Brett's pectoral through his shirt, Nedrick could still feel the firmness of the muscle. Unable to help himself, he blurted out, "You feel amazing."

"Uh, thanks," Brett muttered. A second later, he hissed, "Shit," as he tensed in Nedrick's arms.

"What's wrong?" Nedrick barely resisted the urge to peer over Brett's shoulder so he could look down at him. His instinct did have him lowering his gaze, which showed him an enticing peek of the tops of Brett's glorious ass cheeks. Doing his best to focus, Nedrick registered his mate's rough breathing, and the angle of his left elbow told him his mate no longer cradled it toward his chest. "What are you doing?" Holding Brett in place with his palm to his chest, he moved his left hand to grip his mate's left elbow. "Arm up, handsome. You're not supposed to be using that hand."

Nedrick's guess that was why Brett had muttered a curse was confirmed when Brett grumbled, "Can't do up my zipper and button with one hand." With a growl, even as he allowed Nedrick to reposition his arm upward, Brett groaned . . . and it wasn't the good kind of noise. "Damn, that hurts."

"I'm so sorry, my mate," Nedrick soothed, rubbing his cheek against the back of Brett's head. He enjoyed the feel of his human's soft, thick hair sliding against his face. Brett's pleasant scent, regardless of the acrid tinge of pain, called to him on the basest of levels, causing his prick to thicken. "I'm so sorry this happened to you."

While Nedrick knew it wasn't really his fault, he still kicked himself for not sticking closer to Brett, for not being on hand to stop him from falling. Hearing his mate's surprised shout, seeing him tumble from view, had damn near given him a heart attack. Nedrick had scrambled down the slippery slope after his human, his heart in his throat and his pulse racing. Hearing Brett return his call had offered him the greatest relief.

"Just bad luck, I suppose," Brett mumbled, panting softly, obviously trying to get his breathing under control. With a sigh, he murmured, "And being pushed at the wrong bushes."

Nedrick growled under his breath, sliding his left hand back around Brett's waist again. "Damn Karissa." He so wanted to throttle the heartless bitch.

Brett shook his head. "Don't wanna think about it." Instead, his mate seemed to be trying to do up his shorts again.

Nedrick decided to revisit that thought another time.

Maybe when my mate isn't focusing on his shorts. Speaking of which . . .

"If you don't mind, I can help you with that," Nedrick offered.

Freezing in Nedrick's arms, Brett peered over his shoulder and gave him the side-eye. "Help me with what?"

Slowly sliding his left hand down toward Brett's waistband, Nedrick felt a rush of arousal surge through him. While the timing might be inappropriate, he couldn't seem to help himself. For the first time, Nedrick had his mate in his arms, they were alone, and nothing had ever felt so right.

"Help zip and button your shorts," Nedrick offered, easing his left hand to grip the fabric of Brett's shorts. Feeling the slide of a different kind of bulge move across the side of his forefinger, Nedrick sucked in a sharp breath. That was when he smelled it, and he couldn't figure out how he'd missed it before. *Arousal.* His mate was aroused. "Or help with something else," Nedrick whispered into Brett's ear, nuzzling his nose along the side of his neck. "Endorphins are nature's painkillers."

Brett swallowed so hard that Nedrick could actually hear it. His mate trembled in his arms. His right hand moved to grip Nedrick's right wrist at his chest.

"N-Never been, uh, been aroused by a guy like this before," Brett muttered, discomfort and confusion lacing his tone. "But, shit, if you're offerin'."

"I'm offering," Nedrick confirmed, excitement flooding him. "Just relax, lean on me, and let me take care of everything."

After letting out a slow, deep breath, Brett leaned against Nedrick, offering his weight.

Nedrick's wolf howled in his mind at Brett's trusting move. Smiling, he rubbed his lips along his mate's column of flesh. As he kissed over the place where Brett's neck met his shoulder, the place he longed to leave his mark, Nedrick eased his left hand to the elastic band of Brett's underwear. He rubbed his palm over the human's lower stomach, teasing his fingers through his mate's treasure trail, before dipping his fingers beneath the fabric.

Feeling Brett's semi-erect dick slide across the backs of his fingers, Nedrick carded his fingernails gently through the hair at Brett's groin. He heard his mate's breathing hitch. He felt the other man's prick firming up, lengthening and thickening.

"Mmmm, yeah," Nedrick murmured, licking the soft skin beneath and just behind Brett's ear. Smiling at hearing his mate's gasp, he pressed a kiss to that same spot as he wrapped his fingers around his mate's length. "Bet your cock is gorgeous. Feels gorgeous."

"H-How does s-somethin' feel gorgeous?" Brett muttered, his breathing picking up.

Nedrick chuckled. "Don't know," he admitted. "Just does."

Beginning a slow jacking of Brett's cock, Nedrick enjoyed the feel of his silky flesh. His man's bone hardened further within his grip, and when he slid his thumb over the crown, he found it damp. Pausing, Nedrick massaged Brett's frenulum while dipping his thumbnail into his piss slit.

Brett hissed and bucked his hips, his grip on Nedrick's right wrist tightening.

Loving that reaction, Nedrick hummed. He lowered his right hand, causing his new and forever lover to shift his grip to his forearm. Nedrick quickly pulled the elastic band of his underwear forward and down, tucking it beneath his sack. While beginning to stroke his erection once more, Nedrick gently cradled Brett's balls, testing for sensitivity.

"Yesss," Brett hissed, bucking his hips again. He even shuffled his feet a little, widening his stance. "Fuck yeah. Harder."

Nedrick grinned against Brett's neck and did his best to ignore his own aching erection. He obeyed his mate's command and tightened his grip on his mate's testicles before easing the hold and rolling his palm around his sack. The soft cry that fell from Brett's lips, coupled with the way he began rocking in time with his stroking, enflamed Nedrick, and his dick throbbed behind his fly.

Breathing deeply, Nedrick reveled in the heady scent of Brett's arousal as it swamped his senses.

Gripping Brett's balls again, giving them a squeeze, Nedrick felt them draw up. Combined with the way Brett panted, how he dug his fingers into Nedrick's arm, as well as how his cock leaked like a sieve every time he rubbed his thumb over the crown on the upstroke, told the story. His mate was close.

"Come for me," Nedrick whispered huskily into Brett's ear. "Give in to the pleasure I give you." He nipped at his mate's earlobe, drawing a gasp from him. Before sucking on Brett's neck once more, he again urged, "Come for me, mate."

Issuing a low, husky moan, Brett did just that. His cock pulsed in Nedrick's hand as he continued to stroke him. Hot cum spurted, coating Nedrick's fingers. The delicious scent of his mate's seed filled his nostrils.

Letting out a moan of his own, Nedrick shoved his right hand between them. He barely managed to get his own dick out and point it toward the ground before his orgasm rolled through his system. It was a damn good thing he didn't bother with underwear.

For the next several minutes, the only sounds filling the cave was the harsh breathing of them both trying to catch their breath.

Finally, Brett's husky whisper broke the silence. "Did you just get off, too?"

Nedrick chuckled huskily. "Hell, yeah." He pressed another sipping kiss to Brett's neck. "You're so fucking hot."

When Brett didn't reply, Nedrick decided not to make a big thing of it. He moved his right hand to Brett's hip for balance before bringing his left hand to his mouth and licking away his mate's seed, enjoying the slightly salty flavor. Once he'd gotten it all, he balanced his mate on his chest as he tucked himself away.

Returning his hands to Brett, Nedrick pulled his underwear back up and tucked away his mate's prick. He pulled up his shorts and adjusted them on his hips. Carefully, he zipped and buttoned them.

After pecking another kiss to Brett's neck, Nedrick urged his human to ease backward a few steps before helping him back to the ground close to a different section of the wall. He could see the flush on his mate's features and scented the slight hint of embarrassment, but there was satisfaction in there as well. Plus, the heavy-lidded look on his new lover was sexy as hell.

Can't wait to put that look there often.

From a side zipper pocket of the backpack, Nedrick extracted several single-packet wet naps. He opened one and quickly cleaned his hands and forearms. After opening a second, he cleaned Brett's good hand before hesitating.

Meeting Brett's gaze, Nedrick murmured, "I don't want to hurt you." He held up a new wet nap. "Do you want to carefully clean the hand on your hurt arm yourself? Or we can leave it for the doc."

Brett met his gaze, although his expression appeared a little guarded. "Uh, I'll clean it a little."

Nedrick nodded, opened it, and handed it to him. As his mate did that, he grabbed a couple of single-dose packets of painkillers. There were a couple of varieties, and he held them up.

"Got a preference?" Nedrick asked. "Allergic to anything?"

Brett shook his head. "Naw." Then he pointed at the *ibuprofen* packet.

Nedrick tore open two packets, figuring moving his mate out of the hole and down the mountain would need a double dose, and handed them to Brett. His mate tipped them into his mouth, and Nedrick offered him a bottle of water. Brett took it and used it to swallow the pills. Then his mate sighed, settled back against the wall, and continued to sip the water.

As Brett relaxed and Nedrick hoped the meds would kick in a little soon, he inspected the cuts and scrapes on Brett's calves. He found a couple of abrasions that he cleaned up, earning a hiss and grunt from Brett, but other than a couple of scrapes and cuts, Nedrick thought his mate had ended up damn lucky.

"Sorry," Nedrick murmured, glancing at his mate's face. He was pleased to see a somewhat relaxed expression there with only a modicum of pain given away by the pinching of his brows. "I know I should have done this first, but—"

"But I needed to piss." Brett flashed a small smile his way before his attention drifted away again. "It's fine."

Nodding again, Nedrick tucked everything away before sitting across from where Brett rested against the wall. "How are you feeling?"

As Brett inhaled deeply, his shoulders lifted. He let it out through pursed lips before focusing on Nedrick. A smirk curved up one side of his mouth.

"Not too bad, all things considered," Brett told him. He roved his gaze over Nedrick's face for a few seconds, his expression telling him that his mate was thinking. Then he scoffed quietly. "You got great hands."

Unable to help himself, Nedrick grinned. "That's not the only thing I have that's great."

Brett offered a small smile. "Oh, yeah?" he asked as a hint of pink began creeping up his neck. "What else is—"

Before Brett could finish, Preall hollered, "Guys? You ready to get out of there?"

Nedrick winked at Brett and whispered, "We'll discuss this later." Then he rose to his feet and shouted back, "Yup."

Chapter Eight

Even with his teeth occasionally clenching from pain — *ibuprofen* could only do so much for a broken bone — Brett found himself impressed with the guys' ingenuity.

They'd used a length of paracord that someone had had in their backpack to lash together a number of branches they'd gathered. Evidently, someone had also been carrying a foldable hand saw, so they'd been able to cut them into fairly uniform sizes. With them, they'd created a sort of hammock chair, complete with straps to attach to a pair of carrying poles.

Currently, four of the guys — Nedrick, Michel, Luther, and Preall — were carrying him down the mountain.

When Brett had been pulled out of the hole, Karissa had immediately run to him and tried to latch onto his arm as usual. Fortunately, Nedrick had been there to stop her. She'd demanded he get out of the way, but he'd held firm.

Thank god.

With the size of the four men and the chair, there wasn't room for Karissa to walk beside him. Tabatha had urged her to walk behind the group instead.

"Don't worry, Brett, honey," Karissa called, trying to peer between Nedrick and Michel, who were holding the rear of the poles. "I'll take ever so good care of you after the doctor sees you."

Brett could just make out Karissa's strident expression as she looked over Nedrick's shoulder.

"It's just a broken wrist," Brett countered, shaking his

head. "I'll be fine. I don't need help."

As Karissa frowned, Nedrick arched a brow in silent challenge. When Karissa pouted and her face disappeared, the guy smirked and winked. Sighing, Brett did his best to relax and just enjoy the ride.

At first, Brett had tried to insist that he could walk. Of course, that had only worked for about five minutes before he started getting light-headed. It'd been damn embarrassing, so he'd agreed to the ride.

When they reached the bottom and the trail widened, Karissa again tried to push near. Fortunately, a pair of park rangers, as well as the doctor, were there waiting for him. A big blond park ranger with a shaved head told Karissa to stay back. The second one, a just as large black guy, approached with a slender blond man.

The blond sported short, spiky hair and greeted him with a warm smile. "Hi, Brett." He regarded him kindly, his blue eyes holding a wealth of understanding. "I'm Doctor Lark Trystan, but please, just call me Lark." His gaze swept over Brett assessingly. "Looks like you had a bit of trouble today. Don't worry. We'll take you to my clinic, and I'll have you fixed up in no time." Pointing at a large black SUV, Lark ordered, "Nedrick, take him and help him into the middle seat."

Nedrick nodded.

As the four guys stopped beside the SUV, Brett heard the other ranger claim, "I'm Ranger Dixon Holsteen. I'm gonna need to speak with you all and get your statements before you can go anywhere." The rest of the group gathered around him, while Jerry hung back and gave Leo a big hug and kiss, since Leo had been the one to go and call for help.

"But I want to go with Brett," Karissa demanded, resting her hand on her hip. "He's my boyfriend. He may need me."

"I'm sure Brett will call you if he needs anything," Dixon countered. "Now, can you tell me what happened?"

Brett didn't bother listening as several people started talking at once.

"Come on, Brett," Nedrick urged. Sliding his arm around his waist, he helped him from the chair. "Let's get you in and sitting."

Pausing at the door, Brett reached into his shorts pocket and pulled out his keys. "Uh, my *Envoy?*"

"I'll make sure someone drives it back to the campground," Michel claimed, taking the keys. To Brett's surprise, Nedrick handed the big man his *Jeep*'s keys, too, and Michel told him, "And I'll give these to Dixon to take to Declan's."

"Thanks, man," Nedrick replied.

Before Brett could wonder about that, Nedrick urged him into the middle captain's chair on the right side. To his surprise, Nedrick slipped into the back, settling on the third-row seating. Lark climbed into the second chair to his left. He lifted the armrest and turned to face him, a reassuring smile on his face.

"Don't worry, Brett," Lark told him again. "We'll take good care of you." Pointing at the black park ranger who was sliding behind the wheel, he explained, "That's Ranger Declan McIntire, my partner, and we're headed to the clinic I run out of our home. We'll be able to get you all cleaned up, take X-rays, and see what we're dealing with."

As the SUV pulled out of the parking lot, Lark began asking Brett about his medical history.

Nearly two hours later, Brett reclined on an examination bed in a nice-sized upstairs space in Lark's clinic above his and Declan's massive lodge-style home. His left arm was now in a cast from his palm to just below his elbow. Lark had shown him the X-ray, pointing out where his ulna had a break about two inches from his wrist. The doctor had told him he was lucky it was a clean break and that it could take anywhere from four to six weeks to heal.

Brett couldn't believe how exhausted he felt, but even as his eyelids drooped, he wanted a shower even more. He felt grimy from not only the hike and fall but also from the pain-sweats he'd endured. Those were the worst, always leaving him feeling slimy and stinking to high heaven.

Lark entered the room again with a small white paper bag. There was paperwork stapled to it. "This is your pain meds, antibiotics, and instructions," he told him, handing it off to Nedrick, who'd followed the doc into the room. "You can take something for the pain every four hours or as needed. The antibiotics need to be taken morning and evening with food for the next four days until they're gone." Then Lark glanced between them before focusing on Nedrick. "You'll make sure that happens, I presume?" A small smile toyed around Lark's lips, and his blue eyes twinkled as if he knew some big secret.

What the hell? And why is he entrusting me to Ned's care? We barely know each other. Why would the doc expect him to care for me?

While Brett had zero desire to deal with Karissa, he would've thought Tyler would have been the logical choice to help him, but other than receiving a text from his buddy saying he would see him at the campground, Brett hadn't heard from the man.

What the hell is going on around here?

"Of course, doc," Nedrick immediately replied. He pinned Brett with a look that he didn't understand as he stated, "I'll take good care of Brett."

Lark grinned, glancing between them. "Wonderful." Then he reached out and touched Nedrick's forearm, drawing his attention. "And congratulations."

Nedrick grinned. "Thanks." The doctor turned away and headed out of the room, pausing in the doorway to add, "And of course, if you have any problems or questions, my cell number's on the paperwork. Just call."

Brett nodded even as he wondered how many doctors gave patients their personal numbers.

Must be a country doctor thing.

"Okay, Brett." Nedrick crossed to the bed. "Are you ready to get out of here?"

"Yeah." Brett slid to the edge of the bed and eased to his feet. "Let's go."

As Brett found his feet, Nedrick rested a hand on the small of his back, as if ready to catch him if he dropped. It'd nearly happened when he'd exited the SUV. It'd been damn embarrassing.

Fortunately, whatever medicine the doc had given him was stronger than the over-the-counter stuff, and his arm no longer throbbed. Unfortunately, his head did feel a little woozy from it. Brett wasn't a big fan of drugs, but he was willing to take the heavier stuff for a day or two before switching to lighter stuff.

Not my first rodeo.

"Come on," Nedrick encouraged. He stuck by Brett as they headed down a hallway to a lobby-type area. Once reaching it, Nedrick asked, "Stairs or elevator?"

While they'd been waiting for the X-ray results, Nedrick had explained that Lark and Declan had added an addition not too long ago. They'd created a large screened-in porch at the back of the house to support a second-story addition. They'd expanded Lark's clinic while adding an exterior entrance on that side of the house with both stairs and an elevator large enough to handle a stretcher.

"Stairs are fine," Brett claimed, and they headed out into the afternoon sun. Making his way down them slowly, he gripped the railing with his right hand. "Hey, uh, do you know where I can get some plastic bags to protect my cast?" Brett really should have thought of it before. "I could really go for a shower right about now."

"There's some in the bag," Nedrick claimed, holding it up. As they reached the bottom, he eyed Brett with a worried expression. "Not sure you're up for a shower at the campground." Just as quickly, Nedrick grinned. "I know just the thing, though. Come on."

Nedrick led the way to his *Jeep*. The second park ranger—Dixon—had popped into the room to not only take both of their statements but to give Nedrick his keys. The man had even asked Brett if he wanted to press charges against Karissa for pushing him, which he hadn't. He understood that it had been an accident, after all, no matter how possessive and bitchy she was turning out to be.

To Brett's surprise, Nedrick opened the door for him. He even touched his hip, as if ready to help him inside if need be. Once inside, the man grinned as he shut the door.

After hurrying around the hood of his vehicle, typing something on his phone as he went, Nedrick climbed behind the wheel. They both buckled their belts before he fired up the engine. Nedrick turned around in the large driveway and headed onto the road.

"How are you feeling?" Nedrick asked as he drove. "Really?" He gave him a quick searching look before returning his focus to the road. "I can't imagine that you could scrub or pour shampoo with one hand."

Brett grimaced, having not thought of that. "I'll figure out a way to manage."

"You don't have to manage," Nedrick countered, glancing his way again. His voice deepened a little as he murmured, "That's why I'm here. To help."

Confusion flickering through him, Brett furrowed his brows as he eyed him. "How are you going to do that?"

Nedrick smiled widely. "Just leave that to me, handsome." He winked. "Leave it to me."

Uncertain of what to say or what Nedrick was thinking,

Brett lapsed into silence. Soon, Nedrick was turning the *Jeep* into a driveway, and a medium-sized log home appeared between the trees. The graying logs showed off its age, but it appeared to be in great shape. The stone chimney off to the right stretched toward the sky. A large porch encompassed the front with a couple of rocking chairs on one side of the steps and a two-seater swing on the other. Two dormers revealed the home had at least a loft-style second floor.

"It's beautiful," Brett murmured, leaning forward and taking it all in. "Is it really as old as it looks? Or was it built to emulate age?"

Appearing pleased, Nedrick told him, "It was built in the early nineteen-twenties." He parked the *Jeep*, turning off the engine, before adding, "When I bought it, it was pretty run down. It took a few years, but I fixed it up. Modernized the interior, of course." With a wink, Nedrick slid out while saying, "I love modern plumbing and great water pressure."

Brett nodded. He could understand that. He couldn't imagine living in a time before showers and hot water.

"Come on, Brett," Nedrick urged, having rounded the hood and opened his door while he was still checking out the home. "I have something to show you."

Instead of leading Brett into the house, Nedrick headed between the structure and a free-standing garage to the back. There was a large patio that led to a back door. A woodshed could be seen a bit further on with several rows of stacked wood inside it.

Nedrick stopped before a six-by-eight structure attached to the back of the house and opened the door.

To Brett's surprise, it wasn't a storage shed. Instead, he found himself staring into an outdoor shower. There was a bench seat on the left side with rounded corner shelves above it containing several bottles. The large showerhead came out of the back wall to the right and boasted a detachable head.

"Wow," Brett murmured, lifting his brows. "I wouldn't have expected this."

Chuckling, Nedrick placed Brett's bag of meds, which he hadn't even noticed the man had been carrying, on the nearby patio table. "Told you. Love my modern conveniences." Pointing at the woods, Nedrick explained, "I love running in the woods, but I don't like tracking anything inside, so I shower out here first."

As Nedrick spoke, he opened a chest to the left of the structure and pulled out a couple of towels, placing them on the lid after he closed it. He returned to Brett's side and reached for the hem of his shirt. Unable to help himself, Brett tensed and took a step backward.

"Let's be careful so we don't jostle your arm," Nedrick murmured, rubbing his side soothingly. "This is me helping, taking care of you."

Brett couldn't remember the last time someone had offered to take care of him. He was an only child, and his parents weren't exactly maternal. They weren't cold exactly, just disinterested. At least they helped pay for college — fifty-fifty, they'd told him, so he could learn responsibility.

After a nod, Brett allowed Nedrick to work his shirt off him. The man was patient and careful, easing the short sleeve over his cast. He folded the shirt in half and draped it over a patio chair before opening the paper bag. Nedrick returned a moment later with a plastic bag and a rubber band.

Holding out his arm, Brett let Nedrick wrap his cast.

"I'll start the water if you want to kick out of the rest of your clothes," Nedrick stated. "It won't take but a minute for the water to heat."

Without waiting for a response, Nedrick turned and did just that. He twisted a couple of knobs, and the water started.

Brett hesitated, staring longingly at the streaming water. His desire for a shower overrode his reticence at getting nude, and he crossed to the patio. Once he'd unlaced his hiking boots, he toed them off, followed by his socks. Brett paused again with his hand over his fly, but then he realized how ridiculous that was.

The man helped me piss, after all, then felt up everything I got.

The memory caused his neck to heat, and he fought against his rising blush. He quickly unbuttoned and unzipped, then pushed the shorts down. Nedrick turned around just as Brett was peeling off his briefs, and seeing the appreciative gleam in Nedrick's brown eyes, Brett lost the fight with his blush.

"You're spectacular, my mate," Nedrick crooned, his eyes narrowing as he swept his gaze over him appreciatively. "Stunning."

Having no idea what to say to that, Brett hurried past him along the stone path and slipped into the shower. He began closing the door behind him, but Nedrick's hand stopped him. Brett gaped as he watched the other man climb into the spacious shower, naked as the day he was born.

"What are you doing?" Brett would forever deny the squeak in his voice.

"Taking care of you," Nedrick replied, gripping his hips and turning him around. "Just relax and enjoy."

Brett did as Nedrick urged, his mind racing.

Shock. That's gotta be why I'm going along with this.

CHAPTER NINE

Nedrick figured he was sort of taking advantage, but he would take every opportunity to touch his mate and build their bond that he could get. Even recognizing that Brett was probably suffering from a mix of shock and being a little woozy from the meds in his system didn't make him exit the shower. Hell, Nedrick rationalized that the fact that his mate *was* on meds was part of the reason he insisted on showering with him.

Can't have Brett falling and hurting himself in the shower, now can I?

With that thought in mind, Nedrick rested his hands on Brett's waist where he'd positioned him partly under the spray. "There ya go," he rumbled over the sound of the rushing water. "Relax there a sec."

Reaching out, Nedrick moved the body wash bottle off the upper corner shelf. "Rest your elbow here," he urged, gripping Brett's arm and easing it upward. "That'll help keep your bag and cast out of the spray and elevated." Nedrick knew that keeping it out of the way would help with the pain.

Once Brett rested his arm where Nedrick instructed, he grabbed the bottle of shampoo. He poured a healthy dollop into the palm of his right hand before returning the bottle to the lower shelf. Rubbing his palms together to work up suds, Nedrick eyed Brett's beautiful, wet mane of auburn hair.

He could still see bits of dirt and debris in it from Brett's fall.

Damn Karissa for shoving him through those bushes.

It didn't matter to Nedrick that Karissa had no way of knowing what was on the other side of them. She never should have put her hands on Brett like that in the first place. Hell, in Nedrick's opinion, she shouldn't be putting her hands on his mate at all.

Shoving his anger way down deep, Nedrick focused his energy on taking care of his injured mate. "Let's get this all cleaned up," he stated, lifting his sudsy hands. "Tip your head out of the spray for me."

It took a second, but Brett did it.

Smiling, Nedrick settled his palms on Brett's head. Sliding his fingers through his mate's wet hair, he ignored the way his human tensed. Nedrick focused on massaging Brett's scalp and working the shampoo through the man's full head of hair.

Damn, his hair's amazing.

After a moment, Brett relaxed, his head lolling back even more. He had his right hand wrapped around the base of the shower nozzle, perhaps for support or orientation. Nedrick could see that his human's eyes were closed, and his lips were parted. It only took another minute or two of working on Brett for his mate to let out a soft moan of pleasure.

The noise went straight to Nedrick's cock, and he adjusted his stance to make certain his lengthening dick didn't brush up against his mate's ass. He certainly didn't want to freak the guy out. Nedrick knew he'd have to have a conversation with his mate about man-love, but now sure as hell wasn't the time.

"That's the way, Brett," Nedrick encouraged huskily. "Just relax and enjoy." Once Nedrick felt certain he'd worked through Brett's hair enough, he murmured, "Tip your head forward."

To help, Nedrick cradled Brett's nape with one hand and urged his mate's lolling head forward. With a sigh, Brett obeyed. Nedrick began threading his fingers through Brett's hair, rinsing the suds. When they were mostly out, he grabbed the spray handle and lifted it down. Moving it around his mate's head, Nedrick made certain he got the rest of the soap out.

Nedrick returned the nozzle to the cradle, grabbed the conditioner, and gave Brett the same treatment with that.

Once finished with that, Nedrick grabbed the body wash. He debated using a loofah but then decided to skip it. Nedrick wanted to massage the soap into every inch of Brett's skin with his hands.

Squirting a massive dollop onto his right palm, Nedrick again worked up a lather. He hesitated only a second before resting his hands on Brett's shoulders. Easing his palms up Brett's neck, Nedrick began working behind his ears gently with his fingertips while massaging his spine with his thumbs. Slowly, he began working his way down.

When Nedrick reached between his shoulder blades, Brett let out a deep groan. His mate pressed into his fingers, and he realized he'd found a tense spot. Focusing there, Nedrick took a few minutes to work out the knots.

"H-Holy fuck," Brett mumbled before grunting softly. He softly slurred his words as he murmured, "S'good."

Nedrick grinned broadly even as he ignored his twitching shaft. He loved that he'd pleased his mate and couldn't wait to do even more. Once Nedrick felt the tension leave Brett's body and he let out a deep sigh, he moved on to finish his back, pausing when he reached the top of his mate's ass.

No need to freak him out.

Reapplying soap as needed, Nedrick moved on to Brett's arms. After that, he massaged under his pits, grinning when Brett chuckled and twitched, revealing that he was ticklish. Then Nedrick reached around Brett's front and worked his way down his mate's chest. He took note of any reactions indicating hot spots—like when he hissed while Nedrick swiped his thumbs over his nipples or how Brett shivered when Nedrick skimmed his fingers along the grooves of his hip.

Bypassing Brett's groin for the moment, Nedrick knelt on one knee and began working down his right leg. He even went so far as to urge his mate to lift his foot so he could massage the arch and ball of his foot and work between his toes. Then he started up the other side.

Brett chuckled softly before muttering, "You're thorough."

"Mmm-hmmm," Nedrick confirmed, grinning. "You wanted clean, and I'm happy to help with that."

Finally, Nedrick once again reached Brett's ass, and he didn't bypass it that time. He gripped the globes and massaged them. When Nedrick skimmed his soapy thumbs down his human's trench, he heard Brett hiss. He felt him tense, so he didn't linger. Instead, he reached between his mate's legs to cradle his balls and fondle them gently, earning him a bark of surprise, the sound full of pleasure from the man.

Grinning, Nedrick reached around and gripped Brett's dick. Smug satisfaction filled him when he found it standing proudly, thick and swollen. His mouth watered as he gave it another slow tug.

"Can I suck you, Brett?" Nedrick asked huskily, licking his lips. His body thrummed with his need, and he knew his mate would taste divine. "Can I bury your cock in my throat and taste you?"

Brett groaned, a tremble working through him. "Yesss," he hissed. "Yes, please."

Eager to do just that, Nedrick helped Brett pivot. "Sit," he encouraged.

Seeing the tremble in his mate's legs, Nedrick gripped his lover's hips to help him ease onto the bench seat. Brett's erection stood proudly before him — a red swollen shaft of maybe seven inches or so with a girth that would make the perfect mouthful. Nedrick skimmed the backs of his forefingers up Brett's shaft, making it twitch before him as he licked his lips.

Meeting Brett's heavy-lidded gaze, taking in his wide chest as he heaved each breath, Nedrick pinned him with a feral smile.

"Beautiful."

"Me or my dick?" Brett asked huskily.

Chuckling deeply, Nedrick replied, "Both."

Nedrick didn't wait for a response. Pushing between his mate's knees, he bent forward and swallowed his human's cock to the root. He buried his nose in Brett's wet pubes and inhaled his mate's clean, fresh, masculine aroma.

The bark of pleasure that erupted from Brett's throat was music to Nedrick's ears. The way his mate threaded the fingers of his good hand in his hair and tugged sent a burst of tingles to his groin. When Nedrick swallowed around Brett's crown where it was lodged in his throat, his mate let out a guttural growl, and his own balls began to pull tight.

He knew neither of them were going to last long, and he didn't have one problem with that. Not one problem at all.

Moving his free hand to Brett's balls, recalling how he liked them squeezed, Nedrick did just that. At the same time, he sucked partway up his shaft and tickled his frenulum with the tip of his tongue. Then he swiped over Brett's circumcised cock head, pushing into his slit.

"Ned, fuck!"

Brett's hips bucked up, and Nedrick went with it. He allowed his mate to bury his cock in the back of his throat, and he swallowed around it. When Brett's butt returned to the bench, Nedrick followed him down.

His body shuddering, Brett roared Nedrick's name again as his cock pulsed in his mouth.

Nedrick swallowed quickly and eased off a little, allowing the next burst to land on his tongue. He enjoyed the salty flavor, especially when it was added to it by another spurt of seed. Gulping that, Nedrick gently rolled Brett's balls, helping to extend his mate's orgasm.

When the next burst of cream hit his taste buds, Nedrick felt his own balls draw up. He grabbed for the base of his cock, but it was too late. Moaning around his mouthful, he jolted as his own release shot through him with the force of a sledgehammer, causing him to shudder and shake.

Popping off Brett's prick, Nedrick pressed his forehead against his mate's thigh as he moaned and floated on the endorphins of the best damn release of his life. "Shit," he hissed, gasping and trembling. "Oh, holy fuck."

Nedrick didn't know how long later, but he felt fingers tentatively run through his hair. Peeling open eyelids he didn't remember closing, he tried to get his breathing under control. He stayed still under Brett's ministrations, enjoying his lover's first foray into reaching out to him.

"D-Did you just, um—" Brett began roughly, then paused. He cleared his voice and tried again. "Did you just come from blowing me?"

Lifting his head, Nedrick smiled up at Brett. "Yes, I did." He took in his mate's shocked expression and chuckled huskily. "You taste amazing, my mate."

Brett's eyes narrowed. "You've called me that since you met me. Mate." He tilted his head to the side. "Does it mean something other than friend? Because you don't sound Australian."

"It does," Nedrick confirmed, but he knew this was not the time to get into shifters and mates. Instead, he went with, "It's a term of endearment," which was true, even if it only scratched the surface. Fortunately, feeling the cooling water hitting his back saved him, and Nedrick winced. Rising to his feet, he reached behind him and turned off the water. "Time to get out." With a smile, Nedrick quipped, "Hot water's running out."

Opening the door, Nedrick appreciated the warm summer afternoon. He grabbed one of the towels he'd set aside and held it out to Brett. His mate took it and slowly pushed to his feet, holding it against his chest to hang down his front.

Turning away, Nedrick grabbed the second one and began wiping himself down. He did a cursory swipe of his legs and torso before lifting it to his hair. Turning back as he rubbed, Nedrick found Brett's attention focused on his left side.

Nedrick glanced down and figured it was the scar on his left upper thigh, just where it met his hip, that had caught Brett's attention. "Gunshot wound," he supplied.

Brett snapped his attention to Nedrick's face, his eyes wide in obvious shock. "Shit, really?"

Choosing his words carefully, Nedrick rested his towel over his shoulders. "Was out running with friends, and we ran into some poachers." He closed the distance between them and took the towel from Brett. As Nedrick explained, he wrapped it around his mate's hips, figuring he would be more comfortable like that. "They didn't take too kindly to us, and I ended up taking a bullet before the cops and rangers arrived to catch and take custody of them." With a shrug, Nedrick beckoned with a crooked finger before heading toward his back door. "A few weeks of healing and a few weeks of physical therapy, and I was fine."

"There's gotta be more to it than that," Brett countered, shaking his head.

Nedrick chuckled. "Sure, there is." With a wink, he opened his home's back door. "When we get to know each other better, I'll tell you all about it. Come on. I'll get us some clean clothes."

Following Nedrick inside, Brett closed the door behind him. "You're not shy, are you?"

"Around you?" Nedrick peered over his shoulder at his mate and smirked. "Nope."

CHAPTER TEN

As Nedrick drove his *Jeep* toward the campground, Brett still didn't know what to make of the other man's announcement. The man wasn't shy around him, seemingly happy to parade nude in front of him after the shower. He'd even remained naked as he picked out clothes for both of them.

No, definitely not shy . . . at all.

Brett figured that if he was honest with himself, which he always tried to be, the man had nothing to be ashamed of. That was for sure. His frame might be leaner than Brett's own, but it was all muscle.

The man even had a six-pack, which Brett had never been able to achieve. Ever since breaking his leg playing football his senior year of high school, causing him to put on a little weight due to inactivity as he healed, he'd never gotten in that great a shape again. Of course, it wasn't as if Brett had tried to do any sports in college. He'd never seen the point of sparing the time. Instead, just as Brett had admitted to Nedrick when he'd asked, he enjoyed hitting the gym to destress.

Fortunately, Nedrick had had a pair of too-large sweatpants from when he'd had to have bandages on his hip and thigh, and he'd needed more room. They fit Brett comfortably, as did the t-shirt the other man had given him. Evidently, Nedrick had ordered it online and the size chart was off, so it'd been a bit large on him.

And the man was shot by poachers.

Brett couldn't believe the nonchalant way Nedrick had

shared the tale.

Crazy.

While Brett was tempted to ask for more details, he held back. Nedrick had told him that he would share more when they got to know each other better. Just how much better did Nedrick expect them to know each other?

The man already mapped every inch of my body and had my dick in his mouth.

Just thinking about Nedrick's hands on him, the way he'd kneaded his muscles, combined with the hot pressure of his mouth on his cock, caused Brett's blood to heat and flow south. He couldn't remember ever blowing so fast. Brett figured it had something to do with how keyed up he'd been from the other man washing him.

That had been one sensual shower.

Huh. Does the hand job and blowjob make Ned my lover?

Naw. We were just a coupla guys scratching an itch.

Maybe a vacation fling. Right?

He probably does this with campers all the time.

Brett grimaced at his thoughts, barely registering the trees out the *Jeep's* window. He didn't know why that thought made him want to growl . . . or hurl. While Brett hadn't been considering finding a relationship until after college, the idea of Nedrick being with a whole bunch of random campers definitely caused a case of the green-eyed monster.

Shit. That can't be good.

"Hey." Nedrick's soothing tenor filled the cabin. "What are you thinking about so hard over there?" He moved his hand from the gear-shift for a second to squeeze Brett's thigh. "Everything okay?"

No. No, everything definitely wasn't okay.

"Yeah, yeah," Brett replied instead. He could think about his spiraling thoughts later . . . *much* later. After all, they were pulling into the campground. "Just spacing a little." That wasn't too much of a lie. "Probably from the meds or fatigue from the stress and pain of the day."

"You're in pain?" Nedrick asked quickly, glancing at him with concern. "I think it's a little early for another pain pill. Maybe you'll feel better once you can relax at the camp."

"Yeah." Brett nodded, happy for the out. "That sounds great."

Nedrick glanced at him again with a narrow-eyed gaze that Brett didn't know how to interpret. "Almost there," he said, turning into their camp slot's loop. "Huh."

Brett almost said the same thing. He spotted his *Envoy* ahead, but Tabatha's *Ford* was nowhere in sight. Neither was Preall's SUV, which should've been parked by the next campsite.

"I wonder where they—oh." Brett gaped for a second before snapping his mouth shut. "What the hell?"

As Nedrick parked where Tabatha's car had been, Brett took in their campsite. Clothing was strewn around the area, and the campfire smoldered from some article that had been tossed too close. His single-person tent had been tossed on its side, and the corner of the one that Karissa had been using had caved in.

"Could it have been a bear?" Brett mused as he eased from the *Jeep*, keeping his arm tucked close. "But we didn't leave the cooler here."

Brett had made a point of locking it in his *Envoy* each time it wasn't in use.

Nedrick inhaled deeply, his nostrils flaring. Shaking his head, he narrowed his eyes. "No, not a bear."

"How do you know?" Brett asked as he fell into step beside Nedrick.

"Uh, no empty food wrappers anywhere," Nedrick pointed out. Frowning, he added, "And didn't you keep everything in your car with the cooler?"

"Oh, yeah." Brett nodded. "Right."

Just then, Brett spotted Tabatha and Tyler coming from round their tent. They both carried an armful of rumpled clothes. While Tyler sported a stormy expression, Tabatha appeared worried.

"Hey, guys," Brett greeted, raising his good hand. Looking around in confusion, he asked, "What happened?"

"Karissa happened," Tyler snarled, curling his lip. "Bitch went crazy after Preall received the text from Ned about you going to his place for a shower."

"Don't call her that, honey," Tabatha scolded softly with a sigh.

Tyler frowned, dumping the clothes on a camp chair that already had a stack on it. "Well, what do you want me to call her?" he grumbled. "A jealous homophobic psycho?"

Seeing Tabatha's brows furrow and her cheeks darken, Brett lifted his right hand in placation. "Hey, whoa. Whoa. Let's not say anything any of us will regret." He winced and thrust his hand through his nearly dry hair. "Besides, it's probably my fault anyway. I didn't mean to lead her on by asking her to come. I mean, we'd only been on two dates. We weren't ever really a couple, but I guess it's good I found out early about, uh . . . some of her less desirable tendencies."

Shaking her head, looking sad, Tabatha admitted, "I had absolutely no idea she had such strong opinions about homosexuals." After putting her armful of clothes onto another chair, she began sorting and folding the items. "I mean, she never said anything one way or the other." Tabatha paused, folding a pair of Tyler's shorts. Cocking her head, she mused, "Although, now that I think about it, she always had some other plans any time I asked her to meet up with Charlie and Matt."

"Who are they?" Nedrick asked curiously before crossing to a chair that was on its side. He picked it up and carried it to Brett. "Have a seat, handsome. Rest."

Grateful, Brett settled in the comfortable camp chair while he listened to Tabatha share, "Charlie and Matt are going into their senior year at our college, same as us. They've been a couple since high school. Really nice guys." Her smile turned wistful. "So sweet to see together. They just got engaged and plan to marry after they graduate."

Nedrick nodded. "Well, I'm not folding your clothes, but I'll take a look at these tents." Heading toward the dented two-person one first, he asked, "So, Karissa ended up a little angry after I sent that text to Preall, and she did all this?"

Brett wished he could help, but he was having trouble keeping his eyes open. Instead, he sat there and watched through slitted eyelids as the others cleaned up camp and listened as Tabatha explained. It seemed Tyler kept his jaw clenched, and Brett could see his best friend biting his tongue each time he wanted to interject something not-so-nice.

"Yeah, after reading the text to us, Preall decided he had time for him and Trina to go to the store for more ice and food to grill before you came back," Tabatha shared. Grimacing, she glanced between Brett and Nedrick before quickly shoving a pair of lacy underwear into her bag. "Um, once they left, Karissa started shouting about how she didn't come up here to spend her time with a bunch of, uh, gay guys." Her cheeks darkened as she shook her head. "Anyway, she got up in Tyler's face, asking him if you were gay or if you were a real man."

Grimacing, Brett cracked an eyelid and peered at his friend. "Bet you didn't like that," he muttered, seeing the dark look that crossed his best friend's face.

Yeah, Tyler would have been pissed. Still seems to be.

"Anyway, long story short, when Tyler said it wasn't his fault you decided you weren't interested, Karissa turned on me and began screaming about me setting her up with a fag"—Tabatha lifted her hand in placation—"her words, excuse me."

Nedrick scoffed. "I understand."

"Tyler obviously came to my defense." Tabatha smiled warmly at her man. "Telling her to back off."

Scoffing, Tyler grumbled, "Her yelling at me is one thing. No one goes after you, baby." After tossing a pair of his shorts into a bag, he reached over and squeezed Tabatha's hand.

"So, Karissa started grabbing our bags and flinging our stuff everywhere." Tabatha rolled her eyes and shook her head. "We stopped her before she could go through your stuff, Brett, and that's why ours is everywhere."

"Damn, I'm sorry about that," Brett muttered, shaking his head. "I'm just not interested in her."

"We get it, man." Tyler smirked as he glanced Nedrick's way where he was busy putting the two-person tent to rights. "Your interest has ended up . . . elsewhere."

Nedrick turned and gave Brett a heated look, and he felt warmth start to creep up his neck.

Right. Elsewhere.

"Anyway, after she went after the tents, I gave her my car keys and told her to go home." Tabatha shrugged. "That I'd have Bethany pick up my car from her. She grabbed her bag, roared out of here, and now" — she sighed deeply — "now I'm hoping my vehicle is in one piece when I get home."

"Both Bethany and William will be waiting for her," Tyler assured her. "Even if Karissa has a mind to do something to your *Focus* once she's safely home, they won't let her."

Tabatha's smile held obvious relief as she peered at Tyler. His friend reeled in his woman and planted one on her.

Brett allowed his eyelids to slide shut again.

Damn. I'm tired.

He'd just about drifted off to sleep in his chair when he heard Preall's surprised voice say, "Damn. What happened here, guys? And where's Karissa?"

Brett fell asleep to Tabatha sharing the story all over again.

"Brett, baby."

Brett felt a hand cradle his jaw and scratch his scalp lightly, drawing him slowly from sleep.

"Come on, my mate," Nedrick murmured into his ear. "You need to eat a little something so you can take your evening pills. Then you can go to your tent and sleep."

Blinking open his eyelids, Brett met Nedrick's warm smile. "Hey," he muttered groggily. Seeing the evening shadows stretching across the area, Brett asked, "How long have I been out?"

"About two and a half hours now." Nedrick massaged his nape lightly as he placed a paper plate on his lap. "It's just a cheeseburger with mayo and ketchup. Tyler says you're not a fan of mustard. Plain, I know, but it'll be easy for you to hold with one hand." Drawing away, Nedrick pointed to the right cup holder. "Get eating. Your water is there. I already cracked the seal so it'll be easy for you to take off the lid. I'll be right back with your meds."

"Thanks, man," Brett murmured, carefully picking up his burger.

Even without any extras, the burger tasted fantastic. It didn't take him long to wolf it down. He hadn't even realized he'd been so hungry, but then it occurred to him that he hadn't eaten since breakfast.

"Do you want a second one?" Nedrick asked, holding out his pills.

Brett thought about it as he took a swig of water and swallowed the meds. Then a deep yawn overtook him, and he shook his head. "Naw, I think I'm gonna go conk out." He looked toward where his single-person tent had been and frowned. It wasn't there.

"Sorry, Brett." Nedrick grimaced from where he sat beside him, having obviously followed his gaze. "The ridgeline pole was broken. I suppose I could have used duct tape, but since

Karissa was no longer here, I figured you wouldn't mind just using the other one."

"Yeah, yeah." Brett nodded. "That's fine."

Brett didn't have the energy to be pissed that Karissa had destroyed his property. Although, he probably would be once he was feeling better. It was a shit thing to do—throwing a tantrum like a two-year-old.

On instinct, Brett moved both hands to the armrests in preparation to rise.

"Whoa, nope." Nedrick gripped Brett's right upper arm, staying his action, while sliding his left arm behind his shoulders. "No pressure on that limb now."

"Damn. Yeah," Brett agreed.

Brett allowed Nedrick to help him out of the chair. The other man followed him across the campsite to the tent and unzipped it for him, holding the flap open. Climbing inside, Brett did his best to ignore the small smiles on his friends' faces as they watched.

"Can I return these sweats to you tomorrow?" Brett asked as he eased to a sitting position on the sleeping bag, realizing he was still wearing Nedrick's clothes.

"Whenever's fine, Brett." Kneeling, Nedrick leaned partway into the tent. He pecked a kiss to Brett's lips before holding his gaze and asking, "Do you need help getting in the sleeping bag or anything?"

"Uh, no." Brett licked his lips, and Nedrick followed the action. Feeling a little off-kilter, he whispered, "Um, night."

Nedrick snapped his attention back to Brett's eyes and smiled. "Night, Brett." Then he eased back out of the tent and zipped it up.

Lying back, listening to his friends murmuring on the other side of the tent wall as he waited for sleep to once again take him, Brett wondered what it would be like to have someone who cared so much around all the time.

"No, really," Brett encouraged, smiling at Tyler the following morning. "Don't worry about me." Indicating the tent, he told him, "I'm just gonna crawl back in there and doze all morning." With Tabatha on the other side of their tent brushing her teeth, Brett lowered his voice and told Tyler, "Why don't you take my *Envoy* and go to that place you were talking about? The one with the waterfall?" He lifted his brows meaningfully. "And have that nice time with your girl."

Tyler grinned. "Yeah. Okay." He patted Brett on his upper arm. "Thanks. I'll text you when I know when we'll be back."

"Don't even worry about it." Lifting his casted arm, Brett claimed, "Cast or not, I'm a big boy. I'll be fine."

With a snort, Tyler took his keys and grinned. "See you later."

After they'd left, Brett made sure the fire was banked before he climbed right back into his tent.

Healing sure does take it out of a body.

Brett had just laid back down again when he heard footsteps and spotted a shadow moving outside his tent. At first, he thought it was Preall, but then he remembered that he and Trina had already left.

God, hopefully, Karissa didn't come back.

To Brett's relief, he heard Nedrick softly call, "Brett? You awake?"

"Yeah."

The zipper opened, and Nedrick smiled at him. "Mornin'. Preall told me you were here alone." He slipped into the tent and closed it up behind him.

"Uh, yeah." Brett eyed Nedrick as he rolled out the sleeping bag he'd brought with him. He would forever blame his inane question on his meds. "What are you doing?"

Nedrick grinned and winked. "Relaxing with you."

Brett could just watch, dumbfounded, as Nedrick laid

back, stuffed a jacket under his head, and pulled out an electronic device.

"Ned?" Brett was trying to process what the hell was going on.

Flashing a smile his way, Nedrick reached over and squeezed his right wrist. "Relax and get some rest, my mate," he encouraged. "I'll be here if you need anything."

Then Nedrick pulled up a book on his tablet and started reading.

Uhhhh . . . okay.

With his eyelids once again heavy, Brett decided to just go with it.

CHAPTER ELEVEN

The last three days had been some of the best days of Nedrick's life. He'd spent them with Brett, getting to know him and sharing activities. The only way it could have been better was if Nedrick had managed to figure out how to broach the subject of the paranormal—shifters and mates, specifically.

As Nedrick walked beside Brett, strolling through the woods, he knew this would have to be the day. His wolf was clamoring to get closer to their mate, to mark him and claim him as theirs. Somehow, he would have to find a way not only to share his nature with his mate, but also to explain what his human meant to him—their connection.

To that end, Nedrick had talked Brett into taking a private hike with him to a secluded waterfall that wasn't part of any designated hiking trail. The place was located fairly close to Alpha Declan's home and had been used by many other shifters in the past to connect with their mate. Nedrick hoped it would bring him good luck.

The silence between them was comfortable, relaxed. Neither felt the need to fill their time with unnecessary chatter, but it didn't feel strained at all. To Nedrick, it felt companionable, peaceful.

While walking, Nedrick thought about the last three days they'd shared.

On Monday, Nedrick and Brett had spent most of the day resting. After he'd dropped by unannounced and pretty much invited himself into the tent, he'd wiled away the day caring for his healing mate. For the most part, that meant reading while Brett slept, dozing next to him, and making certain he ate and drank enough to fuel his healing body.

At one point, Nedrick had enjoyed an afternoon siesta. When he'd woken, he'd been spooned up behind Brett, the broader man wrapped in his arms. Brett had patted his hip and asked if he was awake. When Nedrick had responded in the affirmative, he'd muttered, "Good. Wasn't sure I could wait too much longer before needing to get up to use the john."

That had told Nedrick that Brett had woken before him, and his mate had evidently not minded being held by him.

In Nedrick's mind, that had been a huge step forward.

On Tuesday, Nedrick had driven to the campground on his motorcycle. He'd learned from Luther about Brett's interest in exploring the myriad of different home styles in the area. Between him, Luther, Paolo, and Leo, they'd made a list of places to show him.

With Brett mostly sitting on the back of Nedrick's motorcycle, his mate had had plenty of time to rest while enjoying the scenery. There'd only been the occasional walkabout of homes if the owner was pack and hadn't minded them being there. They'd ended the day at a bar in town, meeting up with Preall, Trina, Tyler, and Tabatha, eating great food, and watching their friends play pool and darts. It became a little rowdy when Tabatha had shown off her engagement ring, and there were many who'd offered to buy them drinks. Unfortunately, due to still being on meds, Brett hadn't been able to partake, so Nedrick had mostly held off, as well. They'd still had a fantastic time.

Wednesday, Nedrick and Preall had shown the others one of their favorite fishing holes. Trina and Tabatha had mostly sunbathed. Although they did hop up any time one of them caught a fish to wield the fishing net and help them land their catch.

Nedrick had positioned Brett in a camping chair close by him. Any time he'd managed to catch a fish, he'd encourage his mate to help him. He'd wrapped his arms around him and held the pole steady while Brett reeled it in. They'd had a delicious fish fry.

Being Thursday, Nedrick knew that Brett was only supposed to be there a few more days. His wolf was impatient for him to move things along, and he completely agreed with his animal. Hearing the waterfall in the distance, Nedrick mentally crossed his fingers.

"Hey, is that the river I hear ahead?" Brett asked, breaking the silence. "You said there was a waterfall?"

Nedrick nodded. "Yep. About a twelve-footer. Not huge, but still real scenic." As the trees opened up, he pointed toward the aging wooden buildings half hidden by the encroaching forest. "This used to be a logging camp over a hundred years ago, but times and waterways changed, and the people moved on."

"Oh, wow." Brett paused and peered around at the overgrown, dilapidated buildings. "Is it safe to explore?"

Hesitating, Nedrick glanced at Brett's already casted arm. "Uh." Then, realizing that his mate was a grown man, and he had no cause to curb his desires — plus, the place had been explored to death by so many of his packmates — he nodded. "Yeah. It has the usual dangers of old buildings, rusted nails, broken boards, and so forth, so be careful." With a grin, Nedrick pointed toward the lake the waterfall created. "I'll set up our stuff over there. I'm fancying a swim after that hike. It's hot today."

Wiping sweat from his brow, Brett nodded. "It's a warm one."

"After exploring, maybe you want to join me," Nedrick offered as he started away from Brett. He was so very tempted to lick the sweat off his mate's brow, and while they'd shared a few brief experiences over the last couple of days, Nedrick wasn't certain how Brett would take that action. Instead, he told him, "I brought a bag to cover your cast, just in case." Upon seeing Brett's hesitation, he added, "Even if you just want to wade."

"Yeah, probably." Brett started toward the nearest building. "I won't be long."

Nedrick nodded and started toward the lake. The waterfall was close enough that mist hung in the air, adding to the humidity. The light filtering through the trees and across the water gave the area an almost magical glow.

Perfect.

Dropping the backpack on the ground, Nedrick pulled the blanket off from where it'd been tied to the top. He spread it out before toeing off his boots. Bending, he yanked off his socks and placed them in his boots. Then Nedrick whipped off his shirt and tossed it to the corner of the blanket.

Out of the corner of his eye, Nedrick kept an eye on Brett, watching him poke his head into one building after another. He knelt on the blanket and pulled out several plastic tubs filled with a few items he'd learned Brett liked from their previous picnics and dinners. On top of the towels was a six-pack of soda cans, and he placed them on the blanket, too.

Nedrick had just finished setting everything out when Brett returned. He had a smudge of dirt on his face, and rising, Nedrick couldn't help reaching out to wipe it off. There was also a cobweb in Brett's hair, and he threaded his fingers through it to dislodge it.

To Nedrick's pleasure, Brett chuckled but didn't shy away from him. "Exploring's a dirty business, I guess," Brett stated, rubbing his right hand over his jaw as he held up his left. "So, the plastic bag?"

"Yeah. Let's get you out of that shirt first," Nedrick stated, reaching for the hem of Brett's t-shirt.

As Brett lifted his arms and bent forward, allowing Nedrick to strip him, he muttered, "You like undressing me." His head popped out the hole, and he straightened, arching a dark brow. "Don't you?"

Knowing he needed to go with the truth, as Nedrick eased the shirt over his cast, he nodded. "Yes, I do." Once the shirt was removed, he held it in his hands as he pinned his human with a serious expression. "I'll always enjoy undressing you, my mate."

Brett's nostrils flared as he sucked in a deep breath. His eyes narrowed. For a second, he seemed to be searching Nedrick's face for something.

Then Brett scoffed softly and nodded. "Right. Mate."

Focusing on his feet, Brett began toeing off his shoes.

Watching Brett, Nedrick got the distinct feeling that he'd just missed something. Then, recalling that his human had asked for the plastic bag, he lowered to one knee and fished one out from the side pocket of the backpack, as well as a rubber band. Rising to his feet, Nedrick sucked in a harsh breath as he swept his gaze over Brett appreciatively.

Without prodding, Brett had stripped to a pair of dark red boxer-briefs. His muscular thighs were on clear display, as was his flat stomach and trim waist. The skintight underwear hugged him in all the right places, showcasing a beautiful front-bump.

Nedrick's mouth watered with a desire to drop to his knees and worship that hidden package . . . a package that appeared to be swelling beneath his appreciative gaze.

"Hey, swimming first," Brett stated, moving his casted hand into Nedrick's line of sight. "That's for later."

Wait. What?

Snapping his gaze to Brett's face, Nedrick stared into his mate's green eyes. His breath caught as he spotted the desire swirling in their depths. Nedrick nodded slowly, the realization that his mate intended for them to explore their carnal desires a little later filling him with heady anticipation as his own cock began to swell.

Okay then.

Clearing his throat, Nedrick focused on Brett's arm and carefully banded the bag in place. He hesitated for just a second before reaching for the fly of his shorts. Nedrick couldn't do a thing about his reaction to his mate, especially after a look like that, and he never wore underwear, so he gave a mental shrug and shucked his shorts.

Brett chuckled softly, the sound husky and low. "Right. Never shy around me."

Nedrick paused as he eyed Brett. He found his mate's focus riveted to his erection, which gave a twitch at the scrutiny. When Brett licked his lips, Nedrick barely held in a groan as a fresh rush of heat surged through him, and sweat beaded on his brow for a new reason.

Snapping his attention to Nedrick's face, Brett smiled crookedly. "So, skinny dipping?"

Shrugging, Nedrick admitted, "I never wear underwear."

Jerking a nod, as if Brett was coming to a decision, he shoved down his own boxer-briefs. They'd barely hit the ground before he'd started moving toward the water. His ass muscles flexed and relaxed, entrancing Nedrick.

"Last one in's a rotten egg," Brett hollered over his shoulder, and Nedrick laughed as he rushed after him.

For the most part, Brett waded waist or chest deep, floating a little here and there. Nedrick noticed his mate was always careful to keep his arm out of the water as much as possible. His human eventually grabbed onto the branch of a large tree trunk, which was resting half in and half out of the water. He curled his left elbow around it and relaxed in the water.

Nedrick dove deep and swam to the bottom. He explored behind the waterfall and found a ledge but not a true cave. Standing on the ledge, Nedrick leaped through the curtain of water and dove into the lake on the other side.

The water was refreshing, but it did nothing to temper his need for his mate. It didn't help that, every once in a while, while Brett was floating in the water, Nedrick would catch a glimpse of his human's prick bobbing into view. The crown of the rigid pole would break the surface of the water as if waving at him before Brett sank his hips back under.

If Nedrick hadn't known better, he would've thought Brett was teasing him.

That can't be possible, right?

Nedrick was damn tempted to grip himself and find relief while swimming. Resisting, he decided maybe he could tempt Brett into sharing a rub-off. His mate hadn't touched his dick, yet, but he'd always been more than happy to accept Nedrick's touch.

The prior night in the tent after the fish fry, after Tabatha and Tyler had retired to their tent, Nedrick had curled around his mate and jacked him, and Brett hadn't had any reticence in rocking his ass against Nedrick's erection, helping him get off as well.

One little baby step at a time.

His wolf growled in his mind, telling him to hurry the fuck up.

Swimming toward Brett, Nedrick caught Brett's eye.

His mate smiled at him. "You about done?" Brett asked, arching a brow.

Nedrick nodded. "Yeah." Taking a chance, he stated, "We'll have to come back here after you get that cast off and do this again." Hurrying on, Nedrick continued, "That way, you can swim properly."

Brett swiped his tongue over his bottom lip before saying, "I'd like that."

Relief and pleasure swirled through Nedrick in equal measure. His mate was amenable to thinking about a future together. Nedrick intended to build on that.

"Come on." Nedrick lowered his feet to the bottom and held out his hand. "I brought soda and snacks."

Brett sighed while taking Nedrick's hand. "What I wouldn't give for a beer."

"Not while you're on those strong meds," Nedrick countered, drawing Brett after him. He didn't mention that he might have a few buried under the towels in his bag.

"I'm not on the strong meds anymore," Brett countered, smirking at him. "And I took the last of the antibiotics this morning."

Nedrick frowned. "Aren't you in pain?" He didn't like that idea.

Shrugging, Brett admitted, "A little, but it's manageable." When Nedrick went to open his mouth, his mate told him, "I'm not a fan of medication. Heard too many horror stories about people getting addicted to shit, and I never want to be one of those guys." After a squeeze of his fingers, Brett released him. "Besides, I've seen Trina lift some heavy shit she shouldn't be able to." He smirked at Nedrick. "I wanna know if there are any other perks to being the mate of a werewolf than just increased strength."

Freezing, Nedrick watched Brett continue toward their blanket. Even his mate's enticing ass couldn't get him to move. His brain seemed to be totally stuck.

Brett reached the blanket and flopped back onto it, evidently having gotten pretty comfortable with being naked around him. "Well?" he called. Patting the blanket beside him, he asked, "You gonna tell me? You *are* a werewolf, too, right?" Brett cocked his head and furrowed his brows. "Or are you going to tell me I'm nuts, and I got it all wrong?"

Slowly, Nedrick started forward. His brain began processing again, and he took in the amused expression on Brett's handsome features. Disbelief filled him, beating back his arousal just a little.

Dropping to the blanket beside Brett, Nedrick squinted at him. "You believe in werewolves?" he whispered. "How? Why?" Then Nedrick shook his head quickly, lifting his palm out. He certainly didn't want Brett to get the idea that he was going to go with his last option. "We call ourselves wolf shifters," Nedrick revealed. "Not werewolves, but how did you find out about us?"

Brett nodded slowly. "Okay. Wolf shifters. Makes sense since it wasn't a full moon when we saw Preall change." His tone sounded musing.

"You saw Preall change?" Nedrick jumped on that. "When? How? What happened?" Shocked, he mumbled, "Why didn't he tell me?"

"Because Preall doesn't know we saw him," Brett told him, scoffing softly. "Not the kinda thing you bring up over a coupla beers, right?" Grabbing a soda, Brett waved it in the air and stated, "Hey, Preall, man. We saw you change into a wolf last Tuesday night. Wanna tell us about it?" Smirking as he refocused on Nedrick, Brett shrugged. "See what I mean. Some shit's secret for a reason. Besides, he's not hurtin' anyone." He narrowed his eyes as he mused, "Unless you count the bite scar on Trina's shoulder. Then we noticed the same on Jason and Deke's shoulders when they went swimming, so we figured their partners were ones, too. Does that scar turn you into a werewolf, uh, wolf shifter, too?"

Gods, so many questions, even as he's so very accepting. Where to even start?

Right. Safety first.

"Okay," Nedrick whispered. "First off, who is *we*? And where did you see Preall shift?"

CHAPTER TWELVE

From the look on Nedrick's face, Brett knew he'd gob-smacked the guy. He grinned, figuring he wasn't the only one who had a little explaining to do.

"So, got any beer?" Brett teased.

To Brett's surprise, Nedrick reached over, grabbed the backpack, and rummaged around inside. He drew out two bottles of some IPA that Brett didn't recognize. After popping the cap off both, Nedrick handed him one.

Brett placed his unopened can of soda aside and took a swig. "Huh," he murmured, staring at the label. "Not bad." Then he inhaled deeply, let out the breath, and revealed, "Tyler, Tabatha, and I were walking home from the library late at night last fall. There's a large nature park we have to walk through to get to our dorms. We saw Preall down one of the narrower side paths. We almost shouted to him, but then we saw him take off his shirt." Brett paused, staring at Nedrick. When the man nodded, he continued. "As we watched, Preall stripped the rest of his clothes, tucked them into the bushes, and turned into a wolf."

Scoffing, Brett muttered, "Tyler put his hand over Tabatha's mouth because she nearly screamed." He took another swig of his beer before eyeing Nedrick. "Then the wolf jumped into a pile of leaves that had been blown up against a tree trunk. It rolled around, waving its legs in the air like a dog."

Chuckling, Brett shook his head. "Funniest damn thing I ever saw, especially knowing that the animal had once been

Preall. I mean, the guy's big and friendly, but he can be pretty serious and intense, too. Once the wolf disappeared into the underbrush, we rushed to my dorm room, since I'm in a private one." Holding Nedrick's brown-eyed gaze, Brett admitted, "We vowed not to tell anyone, but to keep watch. We started noticing things after that . . . about Preall and Trina. His devotion to her. Her bite scar. Normally, he calls her love, but every once in a while, he'll use the term mate." Tipping his beer bottle in Nedrick's direction, Brett added, "Just like you do to me." Seeing the questions and concern in Nedrick's eyes, Brett quickly added, "And no, we kept our vow. We've never told a soul."

Brett hummed quietly as he recalled his, Tyler, and Tabatha's whispered conversation at the fish fry the prior evening while Nedrick had been deep in conversation with Preall. "They're the ones that reminded me about the *mate* term and said that the care you've been showing me reminds them of how Preall treats Trina." After a second of hesitation, Brett met Nedrick's gaze again. "So?"

"Well, damn," Nedrick whispered before scoffing softly. To Brett's surprise, he grinned widely at him. "I'm so going to give Preall shit over this." Then his lips softened into a warm smile. "And then thank him." Holding Brett's gaze, Nedrick explained, "A shifter only gets one fated soul mate, which we simply call our mate. That person is the other half of our soul, and if we're lucky enough to meet that person, we do everything in our power to care for and please that person. Yes, Trina is Preall's mate, just as you are my mate." After a second, Nedrick added, "A shifter recognizes that person by scent, and the drive to be with them, to connect with them and bond with them, is damn near irresistible."

Nedrick seemed to be waiting for Brett to say something at that announcement, so he nodded. "Okay. Soul mate." Mulling that for a few seconds, Brett took a sip of his beer. After swallowing, he refocused on Nedrick. "That explains the care Preall gives Trina and you to me. To bond. The scar." Brett slowly talked it out, piecing it together. "You bond by biting and giving your partner a scar. Does that turn them into a shifter, too?"

"No," Nedrick quickly replied. "You have to be born a shifter." Then he winced. "Unless there are illegal government experiments involved." Waving his hand, Nedrick quickly added, "But we won't get into that."

"Ooookay." That didn't sound good, and Brett wasn't certain he wanted to know. Tapping his beer against the inside of his upturned knee, he asked, "So, what does this mean for me?"

After a deep breath, Nedrick began to explain. In halting fits and starts, the other man did his best to lay everything out to him, and there seemed to be a lot. He shared about bonding through sex, biting, and blood. Nedrick explained about increased healing, strength, and extended lifespan.

The news about how anonymity was a shifter's greatest defense made perfect sense to Brett. People could be shit to those they perceived as different.

Just look at Karissa.

Nedrick told him about his wolf shifter pack, the hierarchy, and pack life. Brett was surprised to hear that Declan and Lark were actually the pack leaders. They'd seemed so laid back and down to earth. When Brett learned that wolf shifters were not alone — that there were not only many kinds of shifters out there but other paranormals, as well — he began to feel on information overload.

Through it all, Brett realized Nedrick hadn't answered his most important question. "Hold up, Ned," he murmured, waving his beer bottle — his second one of the afternoon — and the other man fell silent. His expression appeared worried, so Brett quickly asked, "I still need to know. What does this mean for me?"

After a second of hesitation, Nedrick quietly answered, "It means you're the other half of my soul, Brett." His features tightened, turning pensive as he eyed him. "I want to claim you, bond us, build a life together. You and me against the world with my pack at our back."

Brett sat frozen for a few seconds, knowing he should have expected that answer. "And bonding is forever."

Even though it wasn't a question, Nedrick still nodded. Then, as if he was worried Brett would refuse, he stated, "I know humans often need a bit more time, so if you want to date, we can. It's just—" He thrust his fingers through his hair and growled under his breath. "It's just that. You wouldn't be able to date anyone else. Shifters are a jealous lot, and I wouldn't be able to handle scenting anyone else on you. I'd—"

"Hey, easy, easy." Brett touched Nedrick's upper arm, gaining his attention. Once Nedrick's worried gaze was focused on him, he smiled at the other man. "Did you know, watching Preall and Trina together, they're kinda my relationship goal?"

Nedrick cocked his head. "Huh?"

Brett scoffed, smiling and shaking his head. "I mean, I didn't plan on looking for a relationship or partner or whatever until after finishing college, but what they have together's definitely something special." Seeing that Nedrick still wasn't following, Brett shrugged. "Sure, it's a little earlier than I'd intended, but I've really enjoyed our time together these last few days, and now I understand where it's coming from and where it's going. I'd be a damn fool not to grab onto this opportunity with both hands and hang on for all it's worth."

A hopeful look lit up Nedrick's handsome features. "Really?"

And yeah, I can think that now. This man sitting before me is a damn fine man. And I can have him as a devoted lover for all time.

"Yeah, really," Brett confirmed. "I've enjoyed spending time with you. I've *really* enjoyed the way you touch me." Offering a wry smile, he admitted, "You'll find that, for the most part, I'm a pretty laidback, easy-going guy. I've wanted to figure out how to touch you back more than once but hadn't worked up the nerve, but I'll work on that." With a shrug, Brett swept his gaze over Nedrick's naked body and gave him a rakish grin. "Just because you're a guy and not a girl doesn't bother me. It just means I'm gonna have to learn a new skillset is all."

A second later, Nedrick tackled him.

Brett tumbled back on the blanket, a laugh falling from his lips. That died away when he found himself with a mouthful of Nedrick's tongue. The other man delved deep, exploring him, dominating his mouth in sweeping strokes of his tongue.

Relaxing back, Brett happily accepted the ravishing. He moved his casted arm up and out of the way while threading the fingers of his right hand into Nedrick's hair. Brett didn't try to use the hold to take over the kiss. Instead, he relished the opportunity to sit back and enjoy the ride, flicking out his tongue and teasing his appendage against Nedrick's. The other man tasted damn fine, and Brett could easily get on board with enjoying him for . . . well, as long as Nedrick's Fates allowed.

Nedrick broke the kiss and began pressing hot, moist kisses along Brett's jaw to his throat. He licked and nipped at that point where his neck met his shoulder, the place where Brett had seen other people with marks. Understanding slipped through Brett's lust-clouded mind, and he knew that was where Nedrick longed to bite him. Tipping his chin to the side, Brett gave him more access, silently letting his forever shifter lover know he was okay with that.

Yeah, my shifter lover.

Huh. How about that.

Brett smiled, liking those thoughts very much.

The other man's hands seemed to be everywhere, stroking his arms, his rib cage, his stomach. When Nedrick wrapped his fingers around Brett's straining cock, he groaned and bucked. Brett slid his hand to Nedrick's shoulder, doing his best to hang on as he tried to control the pleasure coursing through him.

He wasn't certain how, but every time Nedrick touched him, his body felt as if it burned out of control.

Mates.

Maybe that one word explained everything.

He and Nedrick were connected soul-deep, so everything was intensified.

Then Brett felt Nedrick cradle his balls and squeeze, offering the most deliciously perfect pinch of pain. He gasped and shuddered, the orbs threatening to rise with his impending orgasm. The tingle at the base of his spine shot to his nipples, causing them to bead where they were pressed against Nedrick's chest.

"N-Ned," Brett gasped. "Oh, god." He gritted his teeth, desperately trying to hold on, loving what this man did to him and never wanting it to end. "Fuck!"

Lifting his head from where he'd been working where Brett's shoulder and neck joined, Nedrick peered down at him. Lust and something more filled the man's deep brown eyes. Nedrick's grin appeared feral.

"Can I claim you, Brett?" Nedrick asked, his voice deep and husky as he eased his hold on Brett's balls. "Will you be mine?"

Brett blew out a harsh breath, knowing he had to form words. "Yeah," he managed. After swallowing hard, he told him, "And, Ned, I'm already yours."

Nedrick groaned as he rested his forehead against Brett's. Staring at him intently, he whispered, "My mate." His voice almost sounded reverent. "All mine."

Smiling, Brett murmured back, "All yours."

Lifting up on one elbow, Nedrick roved his gaze over Brett's face. He eased his other hand deeper between Brett's legs, teasing the sensitive patch behind his balls.

Brett hissed, his stomach clenching. He spread his legs a little wider, offering more room.

"Have you ever played with yourself here?" Nedrick slipped his fingers down further, offering a teasing touch to Brett's hole. He pressed ever so lightly. "Explored yourself at all?"

Planting his feet, Brett rocked into Nedrick's touch. "Yeah," he admitted, feeling his cheeks burn for a new reason. Still, he plowed ahead. "I have a vibrating butt plug."

Nedrick's brows shot up. A wide smile curved his lips. "My mate is full of surprises," he rumbled, breaching Brett's entrance with his fingertip. "Still, my cock's a little bigger than the average butt plug."

"Yes, it is," Brett acknowledged. As much as he liked the feel of Nedrick's finger, he had to add, "And unless you have lube in that backpack, what you're packin' ain't gettin' near my ass until we get some."

A warm smile curved Nedrick's lips as he eased away from Brett. "I would never do anything to hurt you, my mate."

Brett nodded, thinking that was it. That they would find their completion another way.

Except, then Nedrick reached over, opened a side zipper pocket, and pulled out a tube of lube. Grinning triumphantly, he waggled it in his hand. Nedrick even wiggled his eyebrows.

"Ready to be mine?" he asked again.

Just as Brett had answered before, he stated, "I'm already yours."

Nedrick groaned and popped the cap. "Normally," he began, pouring a healthy dollop onto his fingers. "I would say hands and knees is best for your first time." Closing the cap, he tossed the tube aside. "But because of your arm, we can't do that." Resuming his position between Brett's knees, Nedrick levered over him and pressed a sipping kiss to his lips before whispering, "So I'll distract you from the burn of stretching and entry another way."

"Oh, yeah?" Brett asked curiously. "How?"

"Like this."

Nedrick captured his lips in another deep, drugging kiss that Brett was more than happy to sink into. As his lover sucked his tongue and explored his mouth, he vaguely recognized the pressure of a finger in his ass. That one became two, but that size wasn't anything he couldn't handle.

Breaking the kiss, Nedrick worked his way down Brett's jaw and back to where his neck met his shoulder.

Welcoming the sucking kisses and nips there, Brett turned his head and wondered if he would end up with a hickey. As that thought took hold, he felt Nedrick press a third finger into his chute. The stretch caused a slight burn, and he grunted softly, doing his best to remain relaxed and pliant.

The sharp sting of teeth sinking into his shoulder caused him to tense despite himself. An instant later, however, the pain was gone to be replaced by the most exquisite ecstasy. Heat flooded him, sending cascading tingles across his chest, down his spine, and flooding his groin.

Brett's cock throbbed, and his balls pulled tight as his orgasm blindsided him. His body was flooded with bliss, his endorphins sending his senses soaring. The sucking on his neck made the sensations go on and on, and Brett could do little but moan and tremble in Nedrick's grip.

Finally, as spots were beginning to flash across Brett's vision, Nedrick eased his teeth from him. When his shifter licked over the wound, Brett hummed and smiled. Even that felt absolutely wonderful.

Nedrick peered down at him, and Brett offered him what

was probably a loopy smile. "Wow," he mumbled. "Could get used to that."

"And how about this?"

To Brett's surprise, he felt Nedrick ease his cock partway out of his ass, only to buck back into him. He gasped as his lover nailed his prostate, sending a fresh wash of tingles through him. When Nedrick did it a second time, Brett groaned, realizing that at some point while Nedrick had been biting him, his lover had replaced his fingers with his dick.

"Yeah," Brett responded on a moan, rolling into the next peg. "Oh, hell, yeah."

Nedrick growled, a look of feral pleasure lighting up his handsome features.

Gripping Nedrick's shoulder, Brett held on for the ride as his wolf shifter began driving into him over and over . . . and what a ride it was.

Yup. Definitely going to get used to this.

EPILOGUE

"You sure you don't want me to come in with you?"
Nedrick asked.

Brett squeezed Nedrick's wrist while shaking his head before releasing him. He wasn't quite at the handholding stage, but he didn't mind a little contact. Brett appreciated that his shifter was patient with him.

"Naw." Brett indicated the wooden benches that had been built around a number of the trees filling his college's courtyard. "Just sit and relax. It shouldn't take me long to pop into the administration office and change my schedule and address." When Nedrick looked doubtful, as if he didn't want Brett out of his sight, Brett laughed. "If there's a line, and I'm going to be more than twenty minutes, I'll text you."

Nedrick sighed even as he nodded. "Deal."

Brett started walking away from the bench where Nedrick was standing. Then he paused and turned back. Girding up his courage, Brett stepped close to his shifter and pecked a quick kiss to his cheek.

Fighting the blush that threatened his neck, Brett muttered, "I'll be back soon."

The grin that spread over Nedrick's face was worth overcoming his slight discomfort.

Brett drew away and started heading toward the building housing the administration offices. As it turned out, the wolf pack owned the building Preall and Trina lived in. Preall acted as the building supervisor for the six-tenant complex. The couple in one of the apartments had graduated, so there'd been an opening for the two-bedroom place. When Preall had offered it to them, Nedrick had insisted they move in together now that they were mated.

Brett hadn't had a good reason to say no, especially since it would save him money. The pack refused to accept rent from pack-members.

"I knew it," a cold feminine voice came from behind Brett, and he paused with his foot on the first step. "I knew you were a fucking faggot."

Turning, Brett spotted Karissa standing ten feet away. She had one hand in her purse and the other clenched at her side. Her face was flushed, and cold fury blazed in her green eyes.

"I can't believe I let you kiss me." Curling her lips into a sneer, she took a step toward him. "I feel defiled, and you're gonna pay for that."

Lifting his hands in placation, Brett countered, "Uh, I'm actually bi, if you want to put a label on it."

Personally, he thought labels were stupid. Why did people need to fit themselves into any particular box? As Karissa took a few more steps toward him, Brett wondered if she was going to try to slap him or something. The college had a zero-tolerance for bullying, and there were others around, so it wouldn't go well for her.

"Look, we had two dates," Brett continued, trying to defuse the situation. "We weren't compatible. Let's just move on," he encouraged. "Bygones be bygones and all that."

"Bygones?" Karissa mocked. "Oh, no." She sneered as she lunged forward, yanking something from her purse. "Payback!"

Pain erupted through Brett's chest as his body jolted, yanking a shocked cry from his throat. Tumbling backward, he dropped onto the concrete steps, his body still twitching. His head slammed onto a stair, as did his casted arm, sending another wave of pain through him.

Then Karissa was leaning over him, and as the sizzling agony returned, what caused it flashed through his shocked brain.

Stun gun.

She's electrocuting me!

Knowing what was happening and doing something about it were two completely different things, however. The excruciating sensations went on and on, as if time were standing still, even though he figured it couldn't have been more than a few seconds.

"Hey! Get away from him," someone ordered as footsteps pounded toward him.

"Brett!" He recognized Nedrick's roar.

Then Karissa was gone, along with her weapon of choice.

Still, Brett couldn't seem to control the way his body twitched and jerked. His limbs were no longer his own, and his head bounced repeatedly against that damn stone step.

"Brett? Baby?" Nedrick was kneeling beside him, leaning over him. "Can you hear me?"

Brett felt his head being cradled in Nedrick's lap, and his wrist was moved to his chest. His body continued to jerk, but the intensity was slowing. He finally managed to suck in a lungful of air, then a bit more, and the spots across his vision began to fade.

Blinking, Brett squinted up at Nedrick, who was running a gentle hand over his face even as he held him steady with the other.

"There you are, baby," Nedrick rumbled, his voice soothing. "You're okay. You'll be okay."

Swallowing hard, Brett managed to get a little moisture into his throat. "Ow."

Nedrick barked a strained laugh. "Ow. Yeah, ow." He glanced to the left, anger flashing across his features before he refocused on Brett, and his expression softened. "Crazy bitch is restrained. Campus patrol has her cuffed."

"Hi, sir. I'm Officer Laura." A young blonde woman in a campus security uniform suddenly appeared in Brett's line of sight. "How are you feeling? Do you need a medic?"

"No," Brett muttered. "I just need a minute." Thanks to having bonded with Nedrick a couple of weeks prior, he could already feel his headache easing. After another minute, Brett tried to ease into a sitting position and appreciated Nedrick's support. "Damn, that was a surprise."

"Can you tell me your name and what happened?" Officer Laura asked, appearing concerned as she looked from Brett to where he saw Karissa was being held in zip-tie cuffs by another officer. "I can get you a bottle of water if you need it."

"I'll tell you what happened," Karissa screamed, trying to tug away from the guy holding her. "He's a fucking faggot, and he kissed me. He defiled me!" Her face was red with rage as she continued to rant. "He should be locked up for touching me with his perverse lips."

"Huh?" Officer Laura looked confused.

"M'name's Brett. Brett Robinson, and I'm bi," Brett told Officer Laura, deciding to keep it brief. "I dated Karissa twice. Realized we weren't a good fit." With a sigh, he explained, "I met Ned here, and Karissa took exception to me dating a guy." Grimacing, Brett shook his head as he watched the officer take notes. "I didn't know she was a homophobe when I met her. Neither did our friends."

"Do you want to press charges?" Officer Laura asked.

"Hell, yeah," Brett replied, noticing a cop car was pulling into the nearby parking lot. Glancing at his wrist, he wondered if he could ask Dixon if he could change his mind about adding charges for his fall, too.

Something to look into.

"We'll get her taken into custody and booked," Officer Laura assured him. "The police may need you to come and make a statement."

"I'll be happy to," Brett claimed, watching as a still-screaming Karissa was transferred to police custody and taken away. A thought came to him, and he commented, "I think she's a student here."

The blonde officer scoffed. "Not anymore. She'll be expelled for this." Shaking her head, she frowned in disgust. "Hate crimes are prosecuted to the fullest extent."

"Good," Nedrick growled. "As they should be."

"Exactly." After jotting down Brett's information, Officer Laura offered her card. "If we need anything, Brett, we'll be in touch."

"Thank you." Brett hesitated, uncertain if he could get his fingers to cooperate, yet, so he was grateful when Nedrick took the card and slid it into his pocket.

"Again, we're sorry this happened, sir," Officer Laura told him before heading to confer with her partner.

"Let's go home, baby," Nedrick urged, helping Brett get to his feet. "We'll come back and do this another day."

Still feeling a little unsteady, Brett nodded. "I'm all for that." As he allowed his wolf shifter to help him back to their car, he grinned over at him. "Hey."

Nedrick gave him a searching look. "Yeah? Need something?"

"At least I didn't piss myself," Brett quipped with a grin. "Heard that can happen sometimes."

Snorting, Nedrick rolled his eyes. "Yes. Yes, that's important."

"And all I need is you, Ned," Brett continued, sobering. "You stole my heart."

Pausing, Nedrick pressed a kiss to his temple and whispered, "And I'll take good care of it."

"I know you will."

Brett smiled as they headed to Nedrick's *Jeep*, safe in the knowledge that he was right where he belonged, in his wolf's arms.

About the Author

Charlie started writing fantasy when she was eight, and after stumbling onto her first erotic romance at age nineteen, she realized her true calling. She now focuses on writing gay erotic romance, normally of the paranormal variety, with heroes of all kinds. With the help and support of her husband, Charlie finally fulfilled one of her life-long goals . . . move to acreage with her horses. You can often find her curled up with her laptop and a cup of tea or glass of wine, creating her next adventure. Charlie enjoys exploring the mountains of her new Oregon home on horseback, 4-wheeler, or motorcycle.

She can be reached at ch.richards2010@yahoo.com

Or visit her at www.charlie-richards.com.

www.ingramcontent.com/pod-product-compliance
Lightning Source LLC
Chambersburg PA
CBHW060646130626
46555CB00002B/985